D1736264

All Plucked Up

Book Two of the Silverville Saga

A Novel by

Kym O'Connell-Todd
& Mark Todd

Raspberry Creek Books, Ltd.

**RASPBERRY
CREEK**

BOOKS

All Plucked Up

ISBN 978-0-9851352-1-8
Library of Congress Control Number: 2012953953

Printed in the United States of America

www.raspberrycreekbooks.com

Raspberry Creek Books, Ltd.
Gunnison, Colorado   Tulsa, Oklahoma

Cover Design by
Kym O'Connell-Todd
Cover Photo by
Larry K. Meredith

Kym O'Connell-Todd dedicates this book
to her brother

Bryan Johnson
(1956-2005)

* * *

Mark Todd dedicates this book
to his father

Dexter Todd
(1918-1990)

Acknowledgments

The authors wish to recognize several individuals who have contributed to the final version of this novel. First, thanks to Kelly Knowles, who checked the colloquial feel of our Spanish. We want to thank Mario Acevedo, Michelle Daily, and Max McCoy – all authors whose work we admire and on whom we relied for thoughtful comments. A special thanks to John Steele and Zac Thompson, who both offered insightful suggestions to strengthen the story's overarching continuity, as well as to Teresa Milbrodt and Marty Grantham for their invaluable close line-edits. We also want to acknowledge Pat Montgomery, who bought his way into the book through a charitable auction and whose real name we turned into a fictitious personality – hope you enjoy what we did to your character! Also thanks to Egan Kelso, who made her chickens available for our research and a photo opp! And finally, warm thanks to Larry Meredith and Raspberry Creek Books, who believed in our work enough to make it one of their titles.

PROLOGUE
August, 1602

Diego Cordova crawled to the edge of the cave and fingered the last of his coins. He'd thrown most of his *reales* at the blood-thirsty *bastardos* before they had begun to torture him. How stupid of them not to realize the value of money. How stupid of his scouting party to think these savages would ever have possessed any gold.

Now he was the only one left to ponder the consequences of such a misguided expedition.

The *indios barbaros* had stripped him of his armor, his finely crafted rapier, and even his boots, leaving him to die at the edge of the valley. He could still hear the laughter of the younger warriors as they loosed random arrows into his half-naked body. Eventually, they seemed to tire of the sport and turned their backs on the carnage of dead Spanish soldiers and their horses. It had given him the chance to gather his possessions and crawl away.

Cordova watched the cave floor grow red with his own blood, some dripping into a dark pool of water near his feet. Why had he volunteered to join the dozen men commissioned by Oñate to explore the uncharted regions above the Rio del Norte? It was a fool's errand, a costly venture that had brought them neither honor nor wealth. Most of his men were lucky, falling swiftly to the first volley of arrows from the ambush. But in his head, he couldn't quiet the last screams of his *compañeros*, or erase the look of terror in Bernardo's eyes just before their tormentors smashed his skull with a rock.

Diego Cordova, proud son of a governor of Spain, could no longer see the stamp of the Maltese Cross on the coin between his thumb and forefinger. Even the light filtering into the cave had become blurred. A rush of anger coursed though him, and he dropped the coin. He was dying and no one would ever know what had become of him. He would never again see his gentle *mamá*, his beautiful betrothed, Carlita. Gone were the tender moments with his beloved Isabella, the finest chicken in all of Spain.

His gut wrenched in spasms. Surely it was not the pinch of hunger that coiled his body into a painful ball – although it had been two days since he'd eaten even a crust of bread. Food had been scarce on the last days of the journey, yet no one was willing to butcher a horse. Not so for the savages. Gusts of wind now carried the scent of roasted horse flesh to his rock shelter as they sang and celebrated their victory on the sides of the arroyo below. Tormented by the heathen lyrics, Cordova clasped his hands to his ears and forced himself to mumble songs from his childhood. Anything to drown the clamor.

"Diego, what are you singing?" a voice asked him.

He stopped and looked up at his father's face, surprised that his vision had become so clear.

"Songs I heard on the street, *Papá.*"

"Do not fill your head with such nonsense."

Then the lovely walls of his parents' *villa* dissolved into the cold granite of the cave, and the horror of the present returned.

Cordova raised his fist and summoned one last surge of defiance. "Damn this God-forsaken wilderness! I curse those who live here. And their children, and their children's children! May they suffer the same indignities as Diego Cordova."

Against the dim light of evening, a sudden flash lit the mouth of the cave. The silhouette of a robed figure limped toward him as Cordova struggled to speak.

"Help me, *Padre*. Can you give me communion?"

The robed figure stooped, reached into his cassock. He placed a small wafer on the conquistador's tongue.

The host tasted sweet to Cordova. "I'm dying!" he gasped.

"What is death but moving from one reality to another?"

"Our quest was for nothing."

"A game, my son. And you were only a pawn."

The words echoed off the rock walls as Cordova's eyes closed for the last time.

4

CHAPTER ONE
Present Day

Pleasance stood atop the Pyramid of Kukulcán, hoping to escape the sticky mid-summer swelter. The Yucatán jungle stretched in all directions, islands of stone ruins occasionally interrupting the monotonous green of dwarfed cedar and chakah trees. Trying to ignore the sweat that pooled between her breasts, she focused on the snatches of international babble that drifted from the base of the structure seventy-five feet below her. Chichén Itzá, an archeological wonder, could bake, broil, and roast people from all parts of the world this time of year. Nothing ever changed at the site. The heat, the humidity, the hordes of people. Even the little vender shops still sold the same kinds of ice cream they always had. The locals hawked the same jewelry, terracotta masks, and Mayan figurines. On her first visits, she was charmed by curios for sale along the walkway that connected the museum to the ruins. But that was a long time ago, long before her buying habits had become a little more discriminating.

In an hour, she would meet Tomás by the parking lot when he got off work. She'd caught a glimpse of him sweeping the museum floor when she first arrived, but as usual they avoided eye contact. She shouldn't have been in such a rush to get here. The two-and-a-half hour drive from the Cancún airport had gone faster than she anticipated, and now she could only wait until closing time for her rendezvous.

Pleasance took a swig from her water bottle. Almost empty. Skirting the rim of the pyramid, she stepped into the temple where a Chac Mool and jaguar throne once stood, now displayed in a Mexico City museum. Probably just as well – some enterprising thief would have covertly whisked them away. She turned and started for the stairway on the western side of the pyramid, sweeping past the tourists who clung to the safety rope that aided them during the steep descent. About a third of the way down, she caught sight of an old man leaning on a metal walker, the brim of his khaki pith helmet bobbing with each familiar-looking step.

"Shit," she muttered and darted back up the stairway towards the temple, elbowing past people who moved down the narrow steps.

"Sorry!" Pleasance called out as one of her long yellow braids snapped a man in the face while she bounded upward, two steps at a time. She rounded the temple and ran to the stairway on the north side. Fewer people had chosen this side of the pyramid for the climb since it had no rope. It gave Pleasance the chance to make her way to the bottom without running anyone down.

As soon as her feet touched dirt, she walked briskly toward the Temple of the Warriors. She hugged the line of trees situated to the south of the Group of a Thousand Columns, careful not to walk so fast that she'd attract attention. With any luck, she'd be able to get back to the site's museum without the old man noticing her.

At that moment she realized that in her efforts to use the pyramid as a blind, she'd placed herself on the wrong side of the open courtyard that would take her back. That meant she would have to cut north into the trees behind the warrior temple, bushwhacking past the Sacred Cenoté to reach the museum. She knew better than to let the courtyard get out of sight. Her track record in the jungles of Honduras had nearly been disastrous on a previous buying expedition. At least here the occasional glimpses of bright-colored tourist clothing helped her navigate.

Within fifteen minutes, she reached the outskirts of the Sacred Cenoté, a great sinkhole filled with water that the Mayans had used for human sacrifice. It was one of many wells dotting the jungle. She blended in with a troupe of sightseers, patiently listening to the guide explain the grisly ritual. When the speaker finished, she moved into the group's center and shuffled along the path until she could cut over to the museum.

* * *

6

Pleasance leaned against her rented Ford as Tomás approached.

"¡Hola!" she said. "¿Qué tal?"

"Chido, y tú?"

"De pelos."

With the obligatory pleasantries finished, she switched to English. It would be Tomás's job to translate for her once they reached the village.

"You said it would be worth the trip. What've you got?"

Tomás lit a cigarette and blew a stream of smoke past her armpit. He seemed shorter than she remembered, but most men seemed short to her.

"Good stuff, Señorita Pantiwycke. Ceramic crocodiles, a death mask – "

"Jade?"

"Of course. Also an obsidian dagger, a stone jaguar. Maybe more. They bring much."

She nodded. The jaguar would be too heavy to smuggle out of the country, but she could probably manage everything else.

"One more thing. These are bad men. I brought you a gun."

At this, Pleasance groaned. An unpleasant aspect of her business, but often necessary. It was one of the tools of dealing in illegal antiquities.

"First, one more question," Pleasance countered. "You haven't seen an old guy in a walker come by here, have you? Trying to sell me to you?" The look on his face gave her the answer. "Okay, guess not. Let's go."

They walked over to his rickety pickup truck, where he reached behind the seat and handed her a cloth bundle. Through the wrapping, she could feel the notches of the revolver's cylinder.

"You follow me in your car," Tomás said.

"How far this time?"

"Only a little ways," he answered as the pickup grinded to a start.

They pulled out of the museum parking lot and traveled a short distance down Highway 180 toward Valladolid. But within a few miles, Tomás turned south ahead of her onto a narrow paved road. He slowed as they passed a sign for the village of Xlohil and turned right onto a dirt corridor cutting through the jungle trees.

Every so often, a little shanty stood off the road, its twig-lashed walls housing a large family by the looks of clothes hanging out to dry. Outside one of the huts, she saw a few ragged children playing in a mud ditch, an emaciated dog skulking at their heels. Her Ford bumped along, hitting more ruts the deeper into the jungle she traveled, and at one point the car lurched so hard her head bounced against the roof. As she slammed back down into her seat, her eyes fell on the rearview mirror and she thought she saw the front end of a blue van making the curve behind her.

"Oh, it can't be!" she said aloud. She studied the mirror, waiting for the vehicle to reappear, but saw no sign of it. It must have been a local who lived in one of the shanties.

She rounded a bend where Tomás had already stopped his pickup near a cluster of dilapidated houses. She pulled up behind him and stepped out of the car, tucking the revolver into her belt so that it snugged against the small of her back.

"Is this the village?"

"Only a suburb." He pointed to the various buildings. "Over there is where my nephew lives, and over that way is where my cousin lives."

They walked between the shacks, sidestepping the goat dung and empty cans that paved the way until they approached a clapboard house larger than the others.

"This," Tomás explained, "is the recreation center." Rusted sheets of corrugated metal covered the roof and several whole slats had fallen from the walls. Plastic covered the windows that weren't boarded up, and the door was gone altogether.

As they passed the building, Pleasance saw ripped mattresses through the gaps in the wall. She also heard a woman groaning to the cadence of a rhythmic thumping noise.

"¡Más, más!" the woman screamed.

They continued down the path several steps before Pleasance clutched her business partner's sleeve. "I thought you said that was the rec center. These people were . . ."

He shrugged and kept walking, saying over his shoulder, "Sí, that is recreation for Xlohil."

As the light began to fail, her other senses sharpened. A rich scent of dirt mingled with rotting vegetation. Occasionally, she caught the perfumed whiff of orchids. Buried in the canopy above her head, she could hear the calls of macaws and woodpigeons. They were deep enough into the jungle forest that she knew larger animals stalked nearby. Predatory animals, like the jaguars the Mayans had carved on their stone temples.

Pleasance picked up her pace, her long strides easily overtaking Tomás.

"So tell me who we're about to meet."

"They would not want you to know their names, but I will tell you anyway." Tomás never changed his gait. "There are three of them. The leader is called Mocoso. Short and ugly. Watch him the closest. And there is Lorenzo. You'll know him by his wild, curly hair. He only does what Mocoso tells him."

"And the third?"

"Rizoso. The bald one, fat and stupid."

She nodded, trying to fit names to the descriptions Tomás had given her.

"*Son tres necios*. Three fools. But unpredictable."

A twig snapped behind them and Pleasance wheeled around. Nothing but the gathering dusk. Raw-nerved, she always experienced a surge of adrenaline before sealing a deal. The trees thickened, creating an impenetrable awning over the footpath, and she struggled to keep her toes from hooking overgrown roots. Within fifty yards, they came upon a low-ceilinged shed with a dim light shining through a single open window.

They stopped well short of the doorway, and Tomás called out to the men inside. She saw the silhouette of a man glance through the window, and a few moments later the door opened.

"Let me do the talking," Tomás whispered as they moved forward.

That was fine with Pleasance. She'd always found it useful to let a local liaison make the initial negotiations. More often than not, these characters ended up being petty thieves, undereducated peasants who were more likely to talk to a local than a blonde American woman. Of course, that wasn't always the case.

Once in Bulgaria, she'd dealt with eastern European Mafia types – high-class criminals counting on her contacts to broker ancient Egyptian stone reliefs to an Amsterdam museum. They may have been too good. They'd already covered the inscriptions with fresh paint so the relics would pass as fakes in order to get them out of the country. When she arranged for one of them to

9

present the artifacts to the museum, the idiot courier failed to remove the new paint and the police arrested him for trying to sell forged pieces. His predicament grew worse when he insisted the reliefs were genuine and all they had to do was remove the paint. That, of course, landed him in jail once Egyptian Antiquities authorities discovered that true artifacts had left the country without proper documentation.

She let Tomás step into the shed's entrance first; she followed, having to duck under the doorjamb.

The short, ugly man – that had to be Mocoso – greeted Tomás and then his eyes grew wide at the sight of Pleasance.

"*¡Qué mujer más grande!*"

Her Spanish was good enough to understand Mocoso's surprise at her size. But the comment didn't insult her. She'd often used this intimidation factor to her advantage. Mocoso's two sidekicks busied themselves further back in the room; with nervous jerks they unpacked boxes. One of them, obviously Lorenzo, arranged some of the loot on a table. He dusted off the priceless jade death mask and placed it under a dirty rag at the far end near the window. At the same time, the other – Rozoso, the fat, stupid one – hoisted a heavy stone jaguar out of an old trunk and set it on the dirt floor. Pleasance moved closer to the objects for a quick survey. Everything looked authentic; she didn't think these three were smart enough to create anything on their own. Tomás had told her that The Three Fools had uncovered a mound at the far reaches of Chichén Itzá at a site that archeologists had not yet discovered in the thick undergrowth. Plausible enough, since the entire area covered over six square miles.

Mocoso leered at her. "You interested in old treasure, *señorita*?" he asked her in fractured English.

She returned his scrutiny and nodded toward Tomás. While her liaison stepped forward and began to barter for the goods, Pleasance became the observer, pretending she didn't know enough Spanish to conduct business. During the course of the discussion, she would point to an individual object and Mocoso would declare its price. After hearing the cost of each, Pleasance and Tomás would retreat to the corner to consider the real value.

"Two hundred pesos," Mocoso announced when she touched a large ceramic bead on the table.

Pleasance pulled Tomás toward her. "That's only twenty dollars. Haven't these guys done this before?"

"They're small-time crooks," Tomás whispered. "Just out of jail. They got seven years for robbing a drive-up bank in Mérida. The teller wrote down their license plate."

Pleasance nodded and they moved the bead aside. She pointed to a sacrificial obsidian dagger with an ornate handle. Lorenzo jumped forward and with great emphasis declared, "Eleven hundred pesos."

Her breath quickened at the proposed price. The dagger would fetch at the very least a hundred times that on the market. But before she could agree, Mocoso leaped at his partner, slapping him across the head and unleashing a volley of colloquial insults.

"No, no, *señorita*. He gives a price too low." He scowled at Lorenzo and turned back to Pleasance. "It is *twelve* hundred pesos."

She nodded again and they moved the dagger near the bead. Next she indicated her interest in a seashell buzzard that sat on a barrel near the door.

"Ah, this one is more, three thousand pesos."

She inspected the buzzard more closely. A number of the shells were chipped and still others missing. She had planned to have Tomás coat the artifacts in plastic and paint them in order to slip them out of the country as reproductions. But the buzzard was sure to lose even more shells in the process. "No, too much. It's damaged."

The three thieves exchanged glances and called Tomás over to them. They spoke in rapid and heated Spanish. After several minutes, Tomás turned to her and said, "They will give you a deal for cash right now."

"Now? No, once we've made the deal, I'll contact my client and meet them again to make the transaction."

At this, Mocoso exploded in anger. Pleasance reached behind her back to touch the reassuring revolver. No one spoke as each of them eyed the others, as though everyone was waiting for somebody to make the first move. Pleasance began to feel like Clint Eastwood in a bad spaghetti western.

She decided she'd better break the silence. "I can have the cash tomorrow, *mañana*."

Mocoso, Lorenzo, and Rizoso moved to the corner behind the table and seemed to debate what to do.

Pleasance leaned over to Tomás. "Are we in trouble?"

"They will likely kill us," he replied in a calm voice.

Before she could comment, Mocoso spoke, "*Está bien. Mañana.*"

Pleasance exhaled with relief. Tomás tried to ease the tension, joking in English, "Ah, women, they have no head for business dealings."

Mocoso started to laugh as did his friends, who obviously had no idea what Tomás had said. With disaster averted, Pleasance looked over at the rag covering the jade death mask on the table near the window. They had saved the best for last, and the most important of the negotiations. She mentally calculated its value on the open market as Rizoso plucked the rag.

His mouth fell open. "*¡Dios mío! ¡La máscara! ¡Ya no la tenémos!*"

Pleasance turned to Tomás. "It's gone?" That was impossible; she'd just seen it earlier when they set it by the window. She began to piece the day together – the old man in the courtyard, the blue van behind her on the road, the snap of a twig on the jungle path.

Where the mask should have been now lay instead a small rectangular purple wafer. She skirted around a wooden box and over to the table, snatched up the little wafer and bit into it.

"Maurice! It was Maurice, that old bastard!"

She sprinted out the door to see if she could still catch sight of him. Behind her, she heard Mocoso call out. "*¡Ladrona!* Thief! Stop her. She has the mask!"

Without thinking, she ducked back inside the door to explain and saw Tomás wrestling a gun from Mocoso's hand.

"Run!" Tomás shouted to her.

But when Rizoso and Lorenzo saw her, they dived in her direction. She snatched the seashell buzzard off the barrel, stuffed it in her pocket, and kicked the drum over to block her assailants. Pleasance turned and ran into the night.

* * *

Brush snapped under her feet as she waded over the dense jungle floor. Clawing through branches and vines, she struggled to place more distance between her and her pursuers. Mud clutched the soles of her boots, pitching her forward into a wall of ferns that tangled in her hair and tore at her braids. The fall terrified her, not because of the tumble but because it could have thrust her face in close proximity to a night-hunting fer de lance – the most deadly snake in the Yucatán. Its venom was so powerful there would be no chance to reach a hospital in time, even if she'd had an antidote. She scrambled to her feet and kept running.

Behind her, angry voices filtered through the vegetation, getting ever closer. Mocoso and his band could more easily navigate the rainforest maze than she since these local *indios* knew the terrain. She needed to get her bearings to help her find the way back to the car. To her right, her eyes caught the reflection of the moon glaring off the damp earth of a narrow animal trail. She dodged down the path, running ten yards before it gave way to a steep embankment. Without warning, she was on her back sliding out of control. She felt the revolver torn from her belt as she dug her heels into the slick mud of a long, sloping hill, fighting to slow her descent. When she reached the bottom, her boots lodged against a low rock outcropping. She struggled to her feet to see the moon shining off a pool of water far below her. A cenoté, its edges rimmed with roots and tree vines that disappeared off the bank and into the watery abyss.

She could tell from the curses and shouts behind her that The Three Fools were now also plunging down the hill. No time to hesitate. She reached for a vine and launched off the edge of the cenoté. She swung blindly into the dark, trying not to think of the bottomless pit of water. For a moment she thought she might escape, but then the top of the vine must have snagged on a limb and she found herself suspended over the well. Before she had time to lament her predicament, her cell phone began ringing.

"Damn!" She wound one arm tighter around the vine so she could free the other to grope in her pocket for the phone. She managed to switch it off before her mud-caked fingers fumbled and dropped the phone into the well.

Just as the phone hit the water, the higher branch hooking her vine broke, and she dropped a dozen feet. Then the jolt of the drop, to her horror, sent the vine arcing backward toward the hill and The Three Fools, and she slammed into the limestone side of the cenoté. Stunned, her grip loosened and she slid down the vine into the pit. But before she reached the water, she landed on a narrow ledge. Pleasance crouched down and tried to hug the wall to stay in the shadows, fighting to slow her breathing so the men couldn't discover her exact location. Tomás had said the black marketeers were dangerous. But he also said they were stupid. She had to find a way to play that against them.

Flashlight beams danced over the vertical rock, but a fringe of dangling roots prevented her pursuers from seeing where she was.

Soon the echo of Mocoso's voice reverberated through the cavernous well. "*Señorita!* You think the vine save you? How long before you fall?"

Adrenaline coursed through her as she crouched on the ledge, and she whirled around, not even sure what she was looking for. Then her foot struck a loose block of limestone.

"Your friend escapes, but not you," a voice called from the rim above.

She reached for the heavy block and finagled it from its resting place. Hefting it above her head, she shouted, "I can't hold on! Help me, I can't swim!" Pleasance screamed as she hurled the boulder into the pool. Immediately, the flashlights angled on the splashing ripples that radiated across the cenoté.

She stayed perfectly still, waiting to see how they would respond. After a few moments, Mocoso called into the well, "*Adios, señorita.*"

Pleasance listened to the clumsy commotion of the men clamoring back up the hill, but she remained silent. An hour later, she began the difficult free climb up the limestone face. Clutching the fibrous vegetation that lined the rock, she pulled herself slowly to the top. Enough light diffused into the forest to guide her back to the Ford. She reached into her pocket for her car keys. Still there, and so was the seashell buzzard. She pulled out the medallion-sized artifact and turned it over until its little abalone wings reflected moonlight. She smiled.

At least her trip wouldn't be a total loss.

CHAPTER TWO

There were two things that Lela most wanted in life. The first was for a decent last name.

Born a Buzzard, Lela endured the usual childhood cruelties from the first day her classmates figured out how to spell. No matter how many times she insisted that her name was BuzZARD, the kids on the playground gleefully called her "BUZZard Girl."

"Hey, you been peckin' at any road kill lately?"

"Buzzard Girl wants a dead rabbit for lunch!"

"It's French, you morons!" Lela would scream.

In retrospect, years of harassment may have built character. Her past experience fighting off kids' taunts taught her never to back down. It gave her the chutzpah to become a tough class president when she was a senior in high school. And it gave her the confidence to argue successfully during college rhetorical debates. All thanks to that horrible last name.

So what'd she do? She married Emmet Schlopkohl.

"Schloppy," as everyone called him, had been a good husband if not a very competent accountant. Each tax season, his customer base shrank a little more as people discovered how he had earned his nickname. His diminishing returns flushed Lela from a life of domesticity and into the workforce, first as an assistant in Motor Vehicles and later as the Silverville, Colorado, County Clerk. Tragedy struck when Emmet ran over himself with his ATV. No one saw it happen, but when they found his body, a perfect pattern of tire tracks imprinted his face and chest. Police said he may have squeezed the brakes too hard as he plowed down a steep slope, upending the four-wheeler and flinging himself in its path.

Just a year later, Silverville elected Lela as mayor. She didn't even have to campaign; she was the only one who hadn't refused the job. Lela passed levies, introduced new city ordinances, and stood up against foolish development plans for three terms. She thought she'd done a pretty good job of weathering the political storms of office until the tourists discovered Silverville's galactic ambience. Hordes of people had flooded the town since Howard Beacon thought he saw that UFO. Some only stayed briefly, hoping for a sighting themselves, while others took up permanent residence. Even her experience as a tough Buzzard Girl had barely prepared her for teacher shortages and overpriced housing – not to mention the Hollywood company now in town to film a movie about Silverville's aliens. At least she'd restored the credibility of the Schlopkohl family name before she stepped down.

And then what did she do? She married Perry Pantiwycke.

They'd met on the golf course at the ninth hole. It was funny that she was attracted to him at all since he was a tourist, wearing a ridiculous Hawaiian shirt. He'd smooth-talked her into a whirlwind romance with his very first words.

"Nice golf shoes."

It also didn't hurt that he was attractive and sophisticated, a well-traveled amateur adventurer. He'd come to town with a group of other retired Rotarians to attend Silverville's first annual golf tournament. As mayor, Lela had played reluctant host at the insistence of City Council. But by the time the day ended, she had a date. They'd gone to the new Chinese restaurant where he used chopsticks with finesse and knew just the right wine for Peking duck. Lela fell under the spell of his commanding voice and confident presence as he told her that he'd made his fortune in the development and manufacture of veterinary supplies, one in particular that brought him considerable wealth – lighted equine rectal speculums.

At the end of the dinner, he excused himself to go to the men's room, and Lela felt her knees grow weak while she watched his straight-backed, long-striding figure walk away. In her eyes, Perry was John Wayne with wavy white hair. She began to imagine how the two of them would appear in wedding photos. He, a tower of manhood, his rugged stature a symbol of self-reliance. She, well . . . short, square.

"You pick good-wooking man." Lela had felt an elbow prodding her side. Her favorite waitress, Kim, gave her a wink. "What his name?"

Yanked from her daydream, Lela turned to Kim and started to speak when the awful realization struck her of how the marriage certificate would appear. "It's . . . Pantiwycke."

Kim stifled a snigger, dropped fortune cookies on the table, and waltzed away.

Several weeks into their courtship Lela started to discover some of Perry's idiosyncrasies. Nothing annoyed her at first, but now after eighteen months of marriage, she'd begun to cringe every time his raucous laughter ended in a porcine-sounding snort.

"It's a family trait," he explained after she begged him to see an ear, nose, and throat doctor. "All Pantiwyckes carry this distinguishing characteristic. You should hear us when we all get together."

Which she soon did, and which was annoying Idiosyncrasy Number Two. Perry loved company, particularly his own passel of Pantiwyckes, who soon made Silverville a favorite destination. She'd opened her home to a procession of relatives named Priscilla, Peter, Preston, Polly, Parnassus, Paul, Paula, Pamela, Pansy, Porter, Patricia, and Poppy.

That was Idiosyncrasy Number Three. All Pantiwyckes began their names with a P, and those not fortunate enough to be born into the family soon acquired nicknames that made them acceptable members of the clan. Even the dog Perry brought to their marriage was a pug named Proust. That explained why he had continuously tested on her a series of endearments like "Precious" and "Pet" – all of which she had soundly rejected.

"I will not have the initials PP!"

No, Lela hadn't succeeded in acquiring a decent last name, and now she was even struggling to retain her first name.

Funny how things sometimes worked out, she thought, as the loaf of bread on the kitchen counter flung itself at her for the third time that day. Which brought to mind the second thing that Lela wanted most in life. For the hauntings to stop.

CHAPTER THREE

Maurice slipped the key into the door's lock and motioned for the taxi driver to bring his luggage inside. Three days' absence was not enough time for his Manhattan brownstone apartment to grow musty, but he wrinkled his nose nonetheless. He maneuvered his walker toward a large overstuffed couch and allowed himself to fall back into the cushions with a sigh. It was always good to get back home. Particularly after another refreshing encounter with Pleasance and the unsavory accomplices with whom she cavorted.

"So where do you want these things?" The taxi driver stood in the doorway, a cumbersome suitcase clamped under one arm and a garment bag slung over the other shoulder.

Nodding his head toward a corner in the parlor, Maurice observed with mild alarm the driver's open fascination with the room's lavish furnishings.

Maurice asked, "Do you like antiques?"

"Not really. It's just that I've never seen a shrunken head on a wall before."

"Ah, dime-store accoutrements. It's made from rubber," the octogenarian lied. "How would a destitute old cripple acquire exotic valuables?"

The taxi driver shrugged.

Maurice rocked forward and rose with ease to grasp the handles of the walker, ushering the man to the door.

"This is for you, my good man," he said, handing the driver a quarter. Without pause he closed the door on the driver's disappointed face.

Rather uncomfortable with the stranger's interest in his possessions, he picked up his carry-on travel bag and glided past a Louis XIV chair next to a Ming Dynasty vase seated on a small mahogany pedestal. Stopping at a locked entrance, he punched the security code into the keypad and listened for the reassuring click of bolts that released the door, which swung open.

He flipped on a light in the windowless room. Even though he heard the hum of the air-handling system, he turned to inspect the readout on the dial hygrometer. A perfect 70 degrees with 50 percent humidity. He set the carry-on down and reached into a small box to retrieve a pair of surgical gloves and snapped them on.

Directing full attention to the jade mask, he carefully lifted it from the travel bag and caressed the green stones. "You'll like living here, but alas, your sojourn will be brief." Maurice thought about the client who would likely purchase the mask. A boorish man. Unworthy, but what could one do? This was, after all, the nature of the game.

"For now, you'll have to take up residence among unfamiliar cousins." He placed the Mayan artifact on a linen-covered shelf between an Eighteenth-Dynasty Egyptian Ushabti and a gilded crown encrusted with lapis lazuli and carnelian stones – both destined to be sold to the highest bidder.

"Thank you, Pleasance, my dear," he said. "At least this time I didn't sell *you* to the highest bidder." He chuckled, amused by his ingenuity. How often had he managed to sell her? Five, maybe six times?

Their first encounter had set a lucrative pattern for Maurice. At the time, they were competing for the purchase of two original Delacroix *épreuves d'artist*. The sketches, initial drawings of a fractious Arab stallion that would figure in *The Moroccan and his Horse*, had been discovered folded behind a mirror by an antiques shopkeeper in Berlin. The sketches soon fell into the illegitimate hands of black marketeers with whom he was already acquainted. Maurice raced to Germany on a client's behalf.

"We've already sold the sketches," they informed him when he arrived at their gallery. They pointed through the window at the Amazonian woman with blond braids who was walking across the street. "To her."

"Has money changed hands yet?"

"*Noch nicht. Morgen.* Tomorrow."

"My client is very rich and powerful. He will outbid anything she offers you."

"You have the money now?"

19

"I can arrange whatever is required."

In the end, they agreed to meet Maurice earlier that next evening at Zum Schwarzen Roβ, an upscale bar in Kreuzberg, where Pleasance had scheduled their transaction.

Maurice arrived an hour before that. And he had a plan. As he entered the establishment, his eyes fell on a table of four well-dressed Japanese businessmen, drinking expensive cognac. Maurice straightened the flower affixed to the lapel of his blue blazer, tightened his apricot ascot, and pushed his walker in the direction of their table.

"*Guten Abend, meine Herren,*" he spoke in expert German. The men replied in passable German, and in a matter of moments he had sold them a beautiful American woman for an evening of entertainment and companionship.

When Pleasance arrived, he intercepted her at the door. "You're here to buy the Delacroixs."

"I'm sorry. Do I know you?"

He gave a slight bow with as much elegance as the walker would allow. "Maurice LeVieux. An associate of the gallery," he lied.

"I don't understa –"

"My dear, the actual owners of the sketches insist on meeting you before we conclude the transaction." He nodded at the Japanese gentlemen seated at the table in the corner, who stood and began chattering among themselves at the sight of Pleasance. "They'll want to buy you a drink before they get down to business," he continued as he pushed her in their direction.

"But I don't speak Japanese," she protested.

"How's your German?"

"Almost nonexistent."

"Don't worry, they'll take care of you."

He shuffled over to the bar and watched for the art dealers. He never had to worry about Pleasance running into the real sellers because the four Japanese businessmen had corralled and ushered her out the door within minutes.

He last saw her looking perplexed as she disappeared onto the street with her eager new clients. Maurice waved gaily at her and patted the tidy sum of cash in his pocket for brokering Pleasance. At eight o'clock, he concluded the deal for the sketches and was on his way.

His tactical diversion had been successful, and by the time he knew she was more than capable of taking care of herself, he managed to devise variations on the Pleasance-as-Prostitute theme on at least four other occasions. He never feared she'd have to consummate one of these arranged transactions. Nevertheless, the distraction did much to slow her down. To Maurice's advantage, poor Pleasance never seemed to see the ploy coming. But she always knew in the end that he had triumphed over her because he consistently slipped her his calling card, a grape-flavored Pez candy wafer.

He crossed the climate-controlled room in the Manhattan apartment, straightening paintings, adjusting shelves of Mayan sculptures, and generally fussing over his very special, if transient, collection.

More permanent, however, was his pride and joy. Treasures so dear that they would never be sold. He carefully unlocked a wall-mounted case, feeling a tingle of anticipation as he beheld an array of little rectangular figurines, each topped with a unique personality. With great care, he lifted the white-bearded head representing a cartoon Asterix character attached to a black plastic mold. Such funny fellows, and perfect choices for Pez dispensers. He abhorred the saccharine little candies that came in those wonderful containers, but he never discarded the wafers. They'd become parting gestures for those unsuspecting few he drew into his games.

Maurice lacked several dispensers to make his collection complete. The elusive Green Hornet, Dino Flintstone and, of course, the rarest gem of all, the Big Top Elephant model. Perhaps one day, Pleasance, who often served as the unwitting legs of his business, would discover a source for the elephant as well. If she did, he would be right on her trail – like he had been so many times before.

* * *

Lela paged through a large book about Colorado history. She stopped and read the chapter on the Spanish Conquistadors and their routes through the southern part of the state. Several accounts described attempts to survey and mine the San Juan Mountains, and some accounts recorded scouting parties who

21

sought out indigenous people already mining gold. However, none
of the documented expeditions seemed to come as far north as
Silverville. All interesting, but Lela didn't find the additional
information she was looking for.

Without warning, something flew past her head and
landed on the floor with a soft thud.

"No, Proust! Bad dog!" she shouted even before turning
around. Right on cue, she heard the habitual clatter of dog claws
race across the linoleum as Proust dived on the bag of bagels that
landed by Lela's feet.

She sighed. Another day of edible missiles. Lela was still
reluctant to label the occurrences of the past two weeks
"hauntings," but what else could they be? Oddly, bread only
seemed to target her and, of course, she'd told no one, not even
Perry. She'd even resorted to going to the grocery store late at
night so people wouldn't see how bread reacted to her.

She pushed Proust aside and scooped up the remaining
bagels. The pug snorted a complaint and waddled to the other end
of the room, leaving a flatulent hiss in his wake before dropping to
the floor.

Thank God for the metal detector Perry had given her for
her birthday. It not only afforded Lela some escape from periodic
episodes of airborne bread but also gave her hours of relief from
the continuous parade of uninvited Pantiwyckes. And treasure
hunting was fun. Sure, most of the things she found were junk – an
old mule shoe, countless tin cans, several buttons. Not exactly
stunning discoveries for two months of prowling around
nineteenth-century mining sites in the backcountry. The most
interesting find she'd come across were three old coins, one found
in a cave among rotted animal bones and two in the arroyo below
the cave's mouth.

Although the condition of the metal made it difficult to
determine the imprints with any certainty, she thought she could
make out large plus signs on one side of each coin. She had even
gone so far as to investigate their origins on the Internet.

"I think they're Spanish!" she'd declared to Perry one
evening while she sat before her computer screen.

"Huh?" He stopped reloading a pocket on his golf bag
with a fresh package of tees and walked over to the computer.

"I think I've found some Spanish coins."

She enlarged an image on the screen to show her husband as she held up one of the actual coins. "Look, don't these seem similar?"

"They *do* look similar."

"It makes perfect sense. When I was a kid, I remember a story about Grady finding some stuff left behind by Spanish explorers."

"Spanish explorers?" His voice became animated. "Some artifacts were found by that old rancher?"

"That's the one. You've met him. Anyway, he'd been bucked off his horse and had to walk back home. Somewhere along the way, he stumbled on a helmet and an old sword. I don't know what happened to any of it, though."

Perry studied first the coin and then the screen. "You're right. They definitely look alike."

"I wonder if they're worth anything."

"I can tell you someone who might know. My niece, Pleasance. Why don't you give her a call?"

"You mean the Pantiwycke I haven't met yet?"

Lela had heard Perry relate countless stories about Pleasance, the jet-setting art historian he'd often taken on vacation when she was a kid. She'd put herself through the first year of college on a wrestling scholarship but soon dropped out to try her hand in the professional ring. To her parents' relief, she'd finally accepted a job with a New York museum. It was there she started moonlighting as an antiquities specialist in her spare time.

So Lela had taken Perry's advice and tried to call his niece, but she'd only gotten an answering machine.

Now, a week later, Pleasance still hadn't called back.

Lela stashed the bagels in the fridge and walked back to the table to retrieve the book on Colorado history. Maybe she should take the coins over to the museum in Denver. Someone there might be able to tell her more. Did Conquistadors leave them here? Was it possible that they left the coins along with the sword and helmet? She found the notion intriguing and decided her next step would be to contact Grady.

Just as she was about to pick up the phone, the doorbell rang. Peering out the front window as she walked to the door, she caught a glimpse of a woman holding a suitcase in one hand and a large covered birdcage in the other.

"Surprise!" the stranger said as Lela opened the door.

Stuffed into a flowered ankle-length dress, the woman marched into the living room and dropped her bag beside the couch and placed the cage on the floor with a careless plop.

"It's me," she announced. "Madame Pompeii."

The name meant nothing to Lela, and she stared at zebra-striped hair only half tucked under a wide-brimmed rose-colored hat.

"I'm Perry's cousin. Didn't he tell you I was coming?"

Lela stammered a greeting but her new guest interrupted. "Sweetie, he didn't, did he? No worries, you won't even know I'm here for the next six weeks."

* * *

As Pleasance entered her darkened New York apartment, she trampled on a couple of envelopes lying just inside. She flipped the switch to see what had been slipped under the door, but the light failed to come on. Enough illumination from the dwindling day filtered through the closed window blinds to let her read the names on the two notices. She tossed one on the table, knowing full well that Con Edison had once again turned off her power. The other she carried over to a window and fully opened the blinds.

That letter, from her landlord, informed her she was now three months in arrears and had ten days to vacate the premises. The notice was postmarked five days ago.

"God dammit!" Kicking a nearby end table, Pleasance gasped as the only lamp in her living room crashed to the floor in several irreparable pieces. But what did it matter? The electricity had been turned off anyway.

She stomped into the bedroom with her bags, throwing them in the corner. Maybe a shower would help. The water would be cold, of course, but with no central air conditioning any kind of relief from the heat would be welcome.

She tugged off her clothes and uncoiled her braids. Slipping into the shower spray, Pleasance faced the water to rinse the sweat from the Cancún jet ride. What a waste of time that trip turned out to be. Her client would be disappointed that she'd returned with nothing but a broken buzzard. Before she left the

Yucatán, she'd tried several times to call Tomás. She knew he'd escaped The Three Fools, and he must be lying low because she hadn't yet reached him. She'd try him again after finding something to eat, but then she remembered that her cell phone was lying at the bottom of a cenoté near Xlohil.

Stepping out of the shower, Pleasance padded into the kitchen without even bothering to dress, the heat and humidity creating an audible slurp from the friction of her naked thighs with each stride. All she'd eaten since boarding the plane were snack packets of barely digestible party mix, distributed by grumpy flight attendants. But when she opened the refrigerator door, a stench of rotting food drove her backwards into the middle of the room. Definitely a night to eat out, and find a pay phone.

On the closet floor Pleasance found a pair of mostly clean sweats and dressed. After tying her sneakers, she left the apartment and headed out onto the evening Soho streets. The scene shared a striking resemblance to the walkway between the Pyramid of Kukulcán and the Chichén Itzá museum. Everywhere along the sidewalk, venders spread blankets laden with jewelry, statuettes of Lady Liberty, and the obligatory fake Rolexes. Scores of people, many of them tourists, shambled among the wares, some munching on hotdogs hawked from nearby stands.

"Excuse us," she heard a husky voice say from behind her.

Pleasance stepped aside for two men dressed in matching bondage leathers. The taller of the two held a chain leash attached to a spiked collar worn by the shorter fellow. Only the out-of-towners stared.

Reaching into her fanny pack, she fished around for some change to buy a hotdog. But the search yielded less than she anticipated, only a few bucks and a subway token. A pretzel would have to do if she wanted money for the pay phone.

Half a block later, Pleasance elbowed her way up to Mr. Ungaro's Pretzel Palace.

"One, please."

"Evening, Miz Pantiwycke." The chubby little man wrapped a sheet of waxed paper around the twist of bread and painted the top with a generous portion of hot mustard. "Haven't seen you around for a few days."

"Been shopping in Cancún," she said, offering a friendly grin. "Just got back."

"Did you go alone?"

She nodded as she paid for the pretzel.

"A pretty girl like you should be married to a nice young man. My nephew, Angelo –"

"A nice young man? No thanks, Mr. Ungaro. I had three chasing me in Mexico, and I hope I never see them again."

Without giving him the chance to respond, Pleasance waved good-bye as she walked away. A half a block down the street, she stopped to look into a shop window. In her peripheral vision, she could have sworn a figure dodged behind a kiosk. She wolfed down the pretzel and continued toward the pay phones.

First things first. She'd check her calls. Certainly, her latest buyer would have left a few messages, eager to get his hands on the Mayan artifacts she'd promised. Sullivan Winchester had been the wealthiest and, certainly, the most enthusiastic client she'd dealt with. So far their relationship had been cordial and cooperative, but she knew how ruthless the billionaire could be when he didn't get what he wanted. She dreaded telling him the news.

When she arrived at the row of phone boxes, she found all five occupied. There it was again – someone in her side vision ducking out of sight. If she hadn't been queuing for a phone, she might have investigated. She leaned against the wall, wondering if she was just feeling paranoid. It couldn't be one of Winchester's errand boys already checking up on her. She'd just arrived back in town, and her client would have no idea about the status of the expedition. She dismissed the notion of being followed when she heard a skinny guy in filthy clothes whine into the mouthpiece of the end phone, "Hey, man, I need the stuff now. . . Yeah, I'll have the money. I just won't be able to give it to you until next week."

Pleasance licked a patch of dried mustard from her thumb, amused that she wasn't the only one who failed to make a deal.

"Well, screw you, too!" the underfed fellow said to the mouthpiece and jammed the phone back into the cradle.

"All done?" she asked, projecting her best New York smile, the one that said, *My turn, get out of the way.*

"Bite me, bitch!" he shouted as he stormed away down the street.

She dropped two quarters into the slot and punched in the number that connected to her messages and listened to an automated voice relay what was in the queue. The first was from Con Edison – she already knew what that was about and deleted it without bothering to listen. She deleted the call from Master Card collections.

The next two were from Winchester. Just as she suspected, he was anxious to know why he hadn't heard from her. He would – as soon as she made her way over to his penthouse office suite. Winchester wouldn't be interested in the troubles she'd encountered, only the end results. The thought of reporting the failure to him made her break into a sweat. For a moment, Pleasance felt like the only other creature besides the lion in a Roman coliseum. She'd have to think on her feet about how to save herself from his eviscerating verbal attack. Or at least she hoped that's all the attack would amount to.

She'd heard worse stories about him.

Partially willing away her trepidation, she listened to the final message.

"This is Lela Pantiwycke," she heard a polite voice begin. "You don't know me, Pleasance, but I'm recently married to your Uncle Perry. He suggested I give you a call to talk to you about some coins I've found. I think they're old Conquistador money. Anyway, would you please call me back when you have a chance so I can take advantage of your, um, expertise?" The woman left her number and hung up.

Uncle Perry. She'd been meaning to call him anyway. Her mind shifted to a scene ten years earlier. Perry was showing her basic wrestling techniques from his college days and had her in a scissors hold with his thighs clenched around her neck.

"What's the third element on the periodic chart?" he shouted.

"Don't know!" she gasped, and the squeeze intensified.

"What's the capital of Nepal?"

"Uncle Perry, I can't breathe." She twisted her head to bite his leg.

"That's the spirit! How many people are dead in the Pantiwycke family plot?"

"Uh, twenty-four?"

"No, all of them." He loosened his grip and let her squirm free. Pleasance crawled over to the edge of Perry's private polo field where the impromptu lesson had taken place.

What a guy, she reminisced as the pay phone queue behind her grew longer. She dialed Lela's number.

* * *

"Yeah, Lela, you could be right about the coins. But you'd need to send a photo so I could tell for sure." But then Pleasance remembered there'd be no place to send a photo if her landlord kept his promise to kick her out in five days. The voice on the other end of the line continued to describe the coins as Pleasance balanced her checkbook. Aside from the negligible remainder of Winchester's travel advance, she had $12.36. And seventy-five cents left in her pocket.

"You say there were other Spanish artifacts found in the area?"

Lela related the story of how an old rancher named Grady O'Grady had years ago stumbled upon a cache of Spanish artifacts. "But they were never recovered," her new aunt said.

Hm. Spanish treasure. Pleasance remembered another Conquistador helmet, intact, that had brought several hundred thousand dollars at Sotheby's the previous spring. If she could convince Winchester that a trip to Colorado might recoup the losses from the Yucatán fiasco, she might talk him into advancing her more travel money to get there.

"Maybe I should come out to Colorado to talk to this Grady O'Grady, or at least assess the value of the coins."

"Oh! No, no, that won't be necessary. I'll just send you pictures."

"Really, it's no trouble at all."

"Let's not be hasty. I couldn't possibly – "

"I can be there within five days. See you soon, Aunt Lela." Pleasance hung up the phone, confident that she could strike a deal with Winchester.

"Planning a trip to Colorado?" a voice asked right behind her.

She looked up as Maurice laughed and started to shuffle away on his walker with surprising alacrity.

"Come back here, you old bastard!" Pleasance scrabbled through the crowd waiting by the phones, and bore down on her crippled prey. She dove in front of him, blocking his path. "You listened to my whole conversation, didn't you?"

"It was hard not to, my dear. Your voice isn't exactly delicate."

"If I so much as even see your face in Silverville, you'll regret your entire miserable existence on this planet."

In his smug way, the old geezer chuckled. "So, it's Silverville. Thank you for telling me."

"What?" The realization of her gaffe pummeled her like a landslide.

She exploded in an exasperated growl and kicked Maurice's walker so hard that it flew from his hands, skidded across the sidewalk, and hit the window of a haberdashery. At the same time, Maurice toppled to the concrete in a dramatic demonstration of shock and pain.

"Shades of Vesuvius! I'm paralyzed," he wailed.

"Oh, shut up. You're more indestructible than a cockroach."

A horrified crowd began to huddle around the prostate figure. Several turned to Pleasance with accusing scowls.

"Look what that woman did to this poor old man!" someone shouted. "Call the police!"

At that, Pleasance turned and hurried down the street before she became victim to vigilante justice. It took a block of city din to distance her from the old charlatan's keening.

* * *

Pleasance stepped off the elevator onto thick carpet. She blinked, adjusting her eyes to the gloom created by dark wood paneling that sucked at the light cast by two lonely Tiffany floor lamps. No windows, no music. She stepped over to the desk.

"Do you have an appointment?"

The secretary's double chin always quivered like the waddle of Pleasance's third-grade teacher. Same unattractive little moustache. And she almost answered, *No I don't have my homework done.*

"Mr. Winchester is a very busy man, you know."

Pleasance looked down at a leather-bound appointment book with no entries.

"Can I wait? He wants to talk to me."

The woman answered a ringing phone and motioned with a bony finger toward a pair of plush chairs against the back wall.

Pleasance sat down and checked to see if they'd added any reading material to the waiting room. The tables were still bare. Not that a person could read in this light anyway.

While she waited, it might be a good idea to figure out how to explain coming back from Mexico empty-handed. She didn't want to end up like Cappelli. His name kept coming back to haunt her. She'd met "Cap" the previous winter at a Sotheby's auction, where they'd both been bidding on the same Pre-Columbian ceremonial headdress. He representing Winchester and she a client who never had enough cash to finance this caliber of transaction. After the hammer came down in Winchester's favor, Cap approached her with his I-want-to-bed-you grin. That led first to drinks at a nearby pub and later a memorable one-night stand. Or so she thought. That spring brought six more dalliances with Cap, each one more passionate than the last. They'd met at predetermined international cities whenever they could arrange the time between her free-lance escapades and his assignments from Winchester.

One day she asked him for an introduction to his boss.

"You don't want to work for him," he said and changed the subject.

Not long after that, Cap disappeared. No messages, no e-mails.

Pleasance was devastated at first. Then pissed. In the end, she pushed it behind her and focused on work, the kind of work that could get her into the major leagues. It took considerable digging, but she found Winchester and decided to hit him up for a job.

Turned out he had an opening.

"Am I filling in for Cappelli?" she asked Winchester. "What ever happened to him anyway?"

"He's gone."

The way he responded made her want to back away. But she didn't, nor did she ask more.

What happened to Cappelli? Had he tried to outsmart Winchester and paid with his life? Was Winchester telling her the truth?

In her own situation, the truth was that Maurice had outsmarted *her*, the Three Fools thought she had double-crossed them, and she had barely escaped with *her* life. But she had learned since then that Winchester cared little for the truth; he operated on lies and dark secrets. Maybe she needed to operate the same way.

* * *

"The artifacts had been moved."

"What do you mean, 'moved'?" Winchester's voice narrowed down to a whisper. He sat behind his desk, flanked by two gorilla-sized goons. He rubbed long delicate fingers across the polished surface of a small glass sphere. The pale skin on his face glowed with the bioluminescence of a deep-sea creature, a sharp contrast to dark violet eyes. To Pleasance, they looked like black marbles set in a distorted snowman's head.

"I got there too late. Everything had already been smuggled across the border."

He paused long enough for her to realize that her nervous bladder felt nearly ready to explode.

Finally, he stood – all four feet, eight inches of him. "Come closer, Pleasance. I want to tell you a little story."

As he stepped around the desk, his two goons bracketed and crowded her forward, close enough to count the dozen gray hairs plastered to Winchester's head. He continued to caress the glass globe.

"Two men, Hami and Noor, once wagered to see who could cross the Negev Desert first. Hami bought himself a fast horse, hoping to reach the finish line before his competitor. When Noor heard of this, he hired spies to enter Hami's camp and break the horse's legs. Deprived of his horse, Hami stole Noor's map, hoping Noor would become lost. But he navigated by the sun and stars. Finally, both men found themselves hours away from desert's edge. But Hami collapsed, his water bag long empty. 'Help me, Noor, and I will let you win the race,' he cried as the other man overtook him. 'I intend to win the race,' Noor replied. 'But first I will offer you a trade for a mouthful of water.'"

Pleasance waited for the end of the story. Instead, Winchester stood motionless.

After thirty seconds, she couldn't stand it any longer. "What was the trade?"

Winchester palm glided forward, holding the globe for her to see. Inside, a severed human ear floated in milky brine.

"And what are you going to trade me to get to the finish line."

Pleasance wiped beads of sweat from her forehead. "Conquistador artifacts."

Winchester closed his fingers around the globe, walked back to his chair, and sat down. "Tell me more."

"I have sources. The artifacts are in Colorado. It wouldn't take much more than a round-trip plane ticket and a few days."

The little man seemed to consider this, and Pleasance began to feel hopeful.

"I'll have funds transferred to your account."

For the first time since she walked into the inner office, her shoulders dropped in relief. It didn't last.

"Let's hope the trade doesn't become a deadly disappointment to one of us."

CHAPTER FOUR

"Good morning!"

Lela opened one eye to see a bulging caftan of purple and yellow waltz into the bedroom. She quickly shut the eye, pretending to be asleep.

"You can't fool a psychic, you know." Madame Pompeii sang rather than spoke her words. "I feel the vibrations of your every thought. Besides, it's the third Wednesday after the summer solstice."

Lela groaned and sat up as the woman placed a breakfast tray on her lap.

"The five-thousandth anniversary of the Druid's completion of Stonehenge."

"What?" Lela stammered.

"The Druids. Stonehenge. Tch, tch. You poor thing, how would you know?"

Then the odor hit her, rising from the tray like a plume of corrosive vapors from an outdoor toilet. Lela gagged as she tried to wave the fumes away from the steaming mug. Small, unidentifiable particles floated on top of the brew.

"What's this?"

"A restorative elixir created from an ancient recipe, revealed to me in a dream. I would have made you toast as well, but I remembered your aversion to bread. But I have to say, I don't think those low-carb diets are good for you."

Lela sniffed the mug. There was something vaguely familiar about the stench. "It stinks. What's in it?"

"Spam's gifts," Madame Pompeii said, her fingers plucking imaginary herbs out of the air. "And a few other things I found in your backyard. Drink it."

Against her better judgment, Lela lifted the mug to her lips and took a tiny sip. It tasted just like it smelled, and she struggled to swallow. "You used Spam in this?"

"Of course not. Not Spam himself. But the gifts that the forest god gives us. You have been visited, my dear. The evidence of his footsteps is all over the back corner of your yard. The small yellow spots in the grass."

Footsteps? Corner of the yard? The only corner Lela could think of was where Proust always went to ... "Oh my God!"

Lela jumped up, spilling the brew on the bed covers.

"Well! I knew it would perk you up, but I had no idea!" Madame Pompeii beamed with satisfaction.

Lela darted down the hall to the kitchen for a cup of coffee to rinse the taste out of her mouth. As she spat into the sink, she heard footsteps shuffle up behind her.

"I hope you have this kind of energy for the journeying tonight."

Lela, still leaning on the sink, turned her head. "Huh?"

* * *

The flicker of thirty candles had transformed Lela's living room into what looked like an opium den. Perry's Watusi masks on the wall and the Massai spear leaning in the corner added to the mysterious atmosphere. A small group of locals clustered in a circle on the hardwood floor. One of them held a drum between her knees.

To Lela, the idea of organizing a drumming circle seemed a bit forward on the part of her new guest so soon after her arrival. But Perry didn't seem offended at all. He'd said his cousin had always been a colorful personality, full of unique ideas, and he assured Lela they'd enjoy the evening. How the woman had been able to round up enough crazy people to participate in all this hocus-pocus was a wonder to begin with.

Perry nudged Lela in the ribs and leaned over to whisper, "This is going to be fun, isn't it, Pom-Pom?"

Lela rolled her eyes, whispering back, "I'm an idiot for letting you talk me into this."

She gazed at the people around her, not surprised to see the New-Ager kooks, Chantale Getty-Schwartz and her so-called spiritual guide, Hans High Horse. Chantale sat in the half-light, applying lipstick like this "journey," or whatever this was supposed to be, was actually going somewhere. Beside her, Hans sat in a lotus position with his eyes closed. What surprised Lela the most, however, were the small number of ranchers' wives who'd come along for the ride.

Just as Lela's legs started to go to sleep, Madame Pompeii swooshed into the living room from the hallway, her robes swirling dangerously close to the candles. A silver star glued to her forehead glittered faintly.

"Welcome, my fellow travelers," she began. "Tonight, our journey will take you to the netherworld and reveal your power animal."

She let her pear-shaped body plop onto one of the cushions in the circle. For a moment, Lela thought Madame Pompeii would tip over backwards, but she righted herself like a bottom-heavy buoy.

"You must let the rhythm of the drumming lead you into a hypnotic trance. Try to think of some familiar hole in the ground – a well or a burrow under a tree – where your mind's eye can follow a path to the netherworld. There you will wait for your power animal to appear."

Perry piped up, "Would a golf hole do?"

Madame Pompeii thought about this for a minute. "Perhaps something a bit deeper so you can travel to the very healing womb of Mother Earth."

"Well, do I go in feet first or head first?"

"I'm going in feet first," Chantale announced, "so my hair doesn't get mussed up!"

One of the other women whined, "I don't like holes. I've got claustrophobia."

Madame Pompeii's voice changed from mysterious to impatient. "You're looking for a pathway for power and wisdom. How you get there is your own business. Okay, are we ready to start? Everyone spread out and lie down flat on your backs and close your eyes." Her voice shifted back into the tenor of a psychic teacher. "Let the drum take you into the Great Mystery."

Everyone shuffled around trying to find a comfortable spot in Lela's tiny living room. Perry situated his legs through the hallway door, so they could stretch out. Madame Pompeii signaled to the drummer, who began a monotonous cadence of BOOM-boom-boom-boom, BOOM-boom-boom-boom.

Perry leaned over and whispered to Lela, "Reminds me of the time I was in the Congo hiding from natives during a tribal ceremony and–"

She shushed, cutting him off. "Yeah, yeah, I've heard that story."

Lela closed her eyes and waited. And waited. Then she remembered she needed an imaginary hole. All she could think of was a mine shaft she'd stumbled upon while exploring for artifacts with her metal detector.

BOOM-boom-boom-boom, BOOM-boom-boom-boom.

But the shaft she'd found that day was blocked with collapsed wooden beams and spider webs. Didn't seem like a promising start for a journey to the Great Mystery.

BOOM-boom-boom-boom, BOOM-boom-boom-boom.

A bigger mystery to Lela was how to get rid of Madame Pompeii. And where was she going to put Pleasance when she arrived? With two visitors in the house, it would be twice as hard to hide the attraction that bread seemed to hold for her. Perry had suggested that they all go out for pizza the night Pleasance flew in. She could see the scene already – dodging foccacia Frisbees that hurtled across the room as they scurried to a table.

A slow, throbbing headache, one that matched the cadence of the drum, began to pulse against her temples. Nearby, she heard Perry's breathing deepen and he began to snore.

She wondered if Pleasance would be able to help her identify the coins she'd found in the cave. She did seem interested enough to travel all the way to Colorado to take a look. Which reminded Lela, she needed to stock up on groceries. Perry said she ate like a horse.

A gasp from across the room startled her, and she opened her eyes in time to see Proust bury his nose in someone's crotch.

"No, Proust, no!" Lela shouted. "Bad dog!"

The drumming abruptly stopped as Proust dashed across the floor, stepping on stomachs and limbs. Everyone sat up except Perry, of course. He continued to snore next to her.

The other journeyers collected once again into a circle.

"Well, let's talk about our experiences," Madame Pompeii said.

Chantale raised her hand. "It was wonderful. I was in the basement at Harrod's. I found an adorable little pin of a buffalo." Chantale sniffed. "It made me think of my poor beloved Tatanka."

Lela still remembered the funeral Chantale had given her big white buffalo two summers ago after Grady shot it for breeding his heifers. She'd never forget the stench of burning buffalo hide when the winds shifted and blew soot from the funeral pyre all over the guests and food.

"Ah, the buffalo. Your power animal signals a time of abundance and plenty," Madame Pompeii explained.

"Golly! If I'd known that, I'd have shopped longer at Harrod's!"

Everyone laughed at this, and finally one of the ranch wives spoke up.

"I decided to use the canning cellar behind our house to go to the, um, netherworld. But all I saw was a rat, so I grabbed a broom and killed it."

Madame Pompeii's mouth fell open. "You killed your power animal?"

She looked around at the group. No one else offered to share their experiences. She turned to Lela. "And did you meet your power animal?"

"Well, I, uh, tried to, um. No, I didn't."

"I didn't think so," Madame Pompeii said. "So I did it for you."

All the members in the circle turned expectant faces toward their journey leader.

"Your power animal, my dear, is a chicken."

No way. Not a chicken. Lela burst out laughing. "I hate chickens! My grandmother had them on the farm. They're disgusting."

Madame Pompeii quickly pulled a manual from her muumuu pocket and paged through it. "Hm, chicken, chicken. No, my book doesn't mention chickens."

She set the book aside and gave Lela a serious look. "But it's what I saw. I don't really know what it means, but it must have some significance."

"Not on your life. It'll never happen."

* * *

Lela put on her trench coat and reached for her purse. She checked to make sure her sunglasses were in the side pocket. Eleven P.M., and safe to go grocery shopping.

"I'm leaving now, Perry!" she called out to the living room, where her husband sat snoozing in front of a blaring TV.

"Oh, okay." He poked his head around the wing of the recliner. "Punkin Pie, why are you always going to the supermarket this late?"

She bit her lip, deciding how to answer.

Perry appeared in the doorway. "Pookie, can't it wait 'til morning?"

"No. Because . . . you're out of cereal."

"But –"

"Never mind. Be back in a few minutes."

A squawking chorus pierced her ears as she ducked out the door. "Watch the bread, watch the bread."

"Damn bird," she mumbled, scowling at Madame Pompeii's gray parrot.

On the way to the store, Lela mulled over the past two weeks of bread bombardment. Obviously, it never happened to Perry and she felt too foolish to tell him about her own experience. She wasn't sure that Madame Pompeii (Lord, when was she going to leave?) had even seemed to notice when the missiles sailed past her very eyes.

Lela turned the corner and saw the lights of the grocery store up ahead.

But why hadn't Madame Pompeii noticed? Her bird, Pandora, certainly had. Every time a biscuit bounced off Lela's head, the parrot would flutter its wings and scream, "Look out! Crust of bread, crust of bread!"

"Don't pay any attention to her," the bird's owner would say. "I never do."

Lela parked the car and walked to the front entrance. A sign announced new, later store hours. She thrust the door open and slipped on her sunglasses. She stopped short when she saw several other customers also wearing sunglasses along with trench coats and turned-up collars.

No one spoke. No one looked up.

Puzzled, she pushed a shopping cart down the aisle, wondering if she'd started a new fashion trend. As she surveyed the shelves, she extracted the shopping list from her pocket and slid the shades down her nose just enough to read. There was more on her list, of course, than just cereal.

For a couple of weeks, she'd confined her trips to the store later at night to avoid the embarrassment. She made her way to the fruit and picked up a few cans of prunes for Perry. Proust needed dog food, so she headed toward the pet supply aisle. From there, she rolled the cart over to the vitamin section to buy another bottle of fish oil for Madame Pompeii. Good brain food, her new relative had told her, but Lela hadn't yet detected any improvement in the woman.

Finally, she reached the bottom of her list and cringed: hot dog buns.

She forced herself to turn the cart in that direction, looking both ways to see if anyone was watching. With a deep breath, she turned the corner, ready to duck at the first doughy volley.

Nothing happened.

Lela pushed her sunglasses atop her head and stared at the shelves of bread, each package of rye, whole wheat, and pita steadfastly ignoring her. She placed one cautious foot after another toward the hot dog buns. Hunching her shoulders in anticipation of the first wallop, she stood on tiptoes and reached for the bag. Her hand froze, still expecting the usual salvo. Again, nothing happened.

Her hand clutched the buns and she threw them in the cart just as she heard someone behind her.

"Ow!"

Lela wheeled around in time to see a package of Kaiser rolls ricochet off the trench coat of another shopper. The victim tore a tin pizza pan out of his cart and brandished it like a shield, dodging a barrage of bakery goods as he continued to pluck items from the shelves. He backed down the aisle in retreat.

Gosh, wish I'd thought of a pizza pan shield. Then it occurred to Lela. *It happened to someone else! Not to me.*

She remained alone in the bread aisle, last man standing – or in this case – last woman, and all was quiet on the wheat-enriched front. Laughing out loud, she whisked off her sunglasses and threw them in her purse. She marched with confident strides to the checkout counter and paid for her purchases.

Before she left, she took one more glimpse down the bread aisle in time to see another trench coat-bedecked target suffer the slings and arrows of muffin militia.

* * *

She dropped the bag of groceries on the table just as Perry walked into the kitchen.

"I'm surprised to see you still up," she said.

"How could I sleep after what happened to me tonight!" Perry's eyes looked as big as his golf balls.

"What?"

"There's something weird going on with the bread."

At that moment, the hot dog buns began rattling in the grocery bag, and Perry jumped back in panic.

With the coolness of a war-savvy soldier loading her gun, Lela opened a cabinet door and handed him her pizza pan. "Here, you'll be needing this."

"No, what I need is a beer."

Lela wanted to say, "This is exactly what's been happening to me." What came out instead was a melodic version of:

"A HUNDRED BOTTLES OF BEER ON THE WALL,
A HUNDRED BOTTLES OF BEER,
TAKE ONE AWAY AND WHAT DO YOU SAY?
NINETY-NINE BOTTLES OF BEER ON THE WALL"

From the living room, Pandora chimed in, squawking, "Sing a song, sing a song!"

* * *

Something unusual was happening in the Pantiwycke home. A demonic entity seemed to be toying with Madame Pompeii's extended family. For the past week, Perry had been the target of poltergeist activity – loaves of bread lobbed themselves at him every time he entered the kitchen. Lela, the poor thing, suffered from some sort of musical Tourette's, frequently breaking out in song.

Fortunately, Madame Pompeii had arrived in time to drive off these evil forces.

But this was proving to be no simple task. To begin with, she'd needed to know the source of the trouble. She had taken her Ouija board into the privacy of an empty closet and asked her spiritual guide, Jim, for help. With both hands on the planchette, she waited for the pointer to slide over the letters and give her an answer. Nothing happened. She tried it again after a breath-cleansing exercise. Either Jim wasn't available or else the dark forces in the house presented a stronger barrier than he could overcome.

Next she'd tried a series of incantations. First a house purification ritual, sprinkling salt water in all the inside corners, nooks and crannies. But she discovered that flatulent dog right on her heels, licking up every drop.

Her only recourse was to find a suitable spell. She paged through her manuals. Nothing on flying bread or musical Tourette's. She'd have to improvise with an original ritual.

For several days, she pondered the problem and finally settled on a combination of shamanistic dance steps with charred bread crumbs. One afternoon when Perry and Lela stepped out, she collected samples of biscuits and hot dog buns. She carried them out to the backyard grill. Now she found a new problem – charcoal briquettes instead of propane burners. After a futile search for a can of gasoline in the garage, she remembered that hairspray was flammable. Madame Pompeii pried the lid off her own can of Aquanet and doused the coals. She tossed in a lit match.

Hairspray *was* flammable.

While she soaked her singed wig and muumuu in the kitchen sink, the coals heated to a suitable temperature for scorching bread. All the better without the muumuu. She'd seen enough television programs on paganism to know that dancing naked always produced better results. She wrapped her blackened head in a towel and went back outside to place the offending items on the grill and began her dance.

Before long, a neighbor's head poked over the next-door fence, asking, "What's for supper?"

No doubt the sight of such a powerful ritual provoked the reaction that followed.

Perry and Lela came home shortly afterwards, bread stuck on his hair and she breaking into song as they walked through the door.

Madame Pompeii would have to find another solution.

* * *

Silverville was a lovely little hamlet, except for its preoccupation with UFOs. Madame Pompeii had heard the now legendary tales of the spaceships that had visited the town, turning the whole community into a mecca for saucer kooks. The first sighting by a single person in the woods was suspect to begin with, and the second she chalked up to mass hysteria. But even Perry believed he'd seen two UFOs above the city park at the Labor Day celebration almost two years before. Still, people often saw what they wanted to, and Madame Pompeii just couldn't abide how gullible some could be. Yes, the answers lay in the stars, but not in the form of little green men.

As she stepped through the entrance of Alien Landing, Madame Pompeii considered the ridiculous nature of the theme park. To partner the psychic booths with carnival rides seemed a travesty, but she felt the need to consult with her own kind. She walked past cotton candy and corn dog stands and bee-lined over to a row of booths and tables that offered everything from Tarot-card readings to aura interpretations. At the far end, she saw a small patched tent bearing the sign, "Arianna's Astrological Astrodome." She opened the flap and entered.

The aroma of jasmine-scented incense floated through the darkened interior. Before her eyes could adjust to the dim light, she heard a woman speak.

"Welcome." The accent was unrecognizable but distinct. "May your soul soon find the illumination it seeks."

Within moments, Madame Pompeii focused on what appeared to be an extraordinarily pale floating head, hovering above a card table. Madame Pompeii took in a sharp, involuntary breath at the sight before she realized the psychic's black dress merely blended with the dark walls of the tent.

"Please be seated." A hand as pale as the head motioned to a folding chair in front of the table. "Would you like an astrological reading?"

"What I'm really looking for is advice." For all Madame Pompeii's bravado, she didn't trust her own abilities. "I'm here on behalf of a troubled couple. As you've probably already picked up, I'm also psychic, but forces seem to be working against all my attempts to help them. I think they're possessed."

"Possessions? That's the last tent on the right."

The astrologer's words sounded like a dismissal, and Madame Pompeii thanked her, got up, and left.

She walked to a tent set apart from the others that displayed the sign, "Kandy-B-Good – Possessions, Auras, and Other Weird Stuff." From outside the tent wall, she could feel the air vibrate with the percussive rhythms of Hip-Hop music.

With much misgiving, she lifted the flap and went inside. Blaring beats from a boom box rattled clusters of pink balloons tied to a Teddy bear seated on a beanbag chair in the corner. Mardi Gras beads dangled from the ceiling.

"Yo! S'up?" An early twentysomething woman with orange and maroon dreads lounged on pillows thrown in the middle of the floor. Sparkling rings adorned each toe of her bare feet.

"Excuse me?"

The young woman turned the music down and held up a lunchbox painted with scenes of Cinderella. "Licorice?"

"No, uh, thank you. I may have made a mistake." Madame Pompeii began to back out of the tent.

"No ma'am, it be manna that bring you here."

"Manna? What are you talking about?"

"Manna. Bread. It making your people crazy."

Madame Pompeii felt her feet dissolve. Kandy-B-Good already knew. Unable to move, she looked down at the strange psychic now chewing openmouthed on a black stick of licorice. Wriggling, jangling toes pointed to an overstuffed fringed pillow. Madame Pompeii sank to her knees and crawled over to it.

Still smacking on licorice, the woman said, "Bread and jingles, it's a problem, ain't it?"

"How did you know?"

Kandy smiled, black chunks sticking to her braces.

The spiritual force of the young psychic's power must have filled the room because Madame Pompeii began to feel a tickling sensation creep along her lower back. She closed her eyes to embrace the moment. If only she could absorb Kandy's remarkable power. Finally, someone who understood the tribulations that had befallen her cousin and his wife. Madame Pompeii squeezed her eyes tighter.

The tickling sensation stopped just as the weight of an invisible presence dropped onto her shoulder.

"Get down, Muffin!" Kandy shouted.

Madame Pompeii opened her eyes in time to see a sleek black cat jump from her shoulder and land in Kandy's lap.

"Bad, bad kitty-cat," Kandy cooed.

The animal stood on its hind feet and rubbed a whiskered face along Kandy's cheek.

The psychic cocked an ear toward her cat's head. "What you say?"

Madame Pompeii stared openmouthed at the one-sided conversation.

The cat began to purr, nuzzling its owner. Kandy nodded, looked at her client, and began to giggle. "You right about that!"

"What did it say?"

"She say your wig be crooked."

Madame Pompeii straightened her hair. "No, what did the cat say about the bread and jingles."

Kandy held up one finger signaling for silence and once again turned her head to the cat. After a moment, she looked at Madame Pompeii and said, "A curse."

"Oh my God! What can we do?" The cat leaped from Kandy's lap, walked over to Madame Pompeii, and stared into her eyes. The long tail flicked once. "What is she trying to tell me?"

Kandy reached for another licorice as she leaned back on the pillow. "Muffin say you find the source, you end the curse."

"How do I find the source?"

"Ya need help." Kandy looked down at Muffin, who had plopped on her side and started licking her paw.

"You mean like a cat?"

Kandy shrugged. "A familiar be one way."

Yes, a familiar, of course. An animal with the power to bridge the gap between the spirit world and the physical plane. She would start looking for a cat just like Muffin.

Madame Pompeii struggled to her feet, thanked Kandy, and pulled several bills out of her purse. The girl pointed to a pink piggy bank.

As she walked out of the tent, Madame Pompeii barely heard Kandy's parting words. "Find the curse. Save the town."

* * *

Sugar! That's what she needed after the emotionally draining encounter with that weird little psychic and her cat. Madame Pompeii walked back past the row of tents and looked for the nearest cotton candy stand. She needed an energy boost.

Where was she going to find a familiar? And how could she be sure it would help her locate the source of the curse? For that matter, she wasn't sure whether any animal would do. The whole familiar idea was a little fuzzy to her. Were they actual animals that became possessed by spirits, or were they spirits masquerading as animals? Well, she'd worry about that after she found her sugar fix.

A few yards up ahead she spotted a pink and white cotton candy wagon, and she fell into line behind a skinny young man. While she waited, she bent over to check her swollen ankles.

"Hi, Howard," a passerby shouted.

She stood back up just as the young man in front of her turned to wave, and she found her face just inches from his.

"Oh, excuse me," he said.

"Quite alright." She stepped back a foot.

The man continued to stare at her.

"You wouldn't by chance be Howard Beacon, would you?" she asked.

He smiled and looked at the ground. "Yes, ma'am."

As he spoke, a little boy wearing a hooded sweatshirt peered from behind Howard's legs. Large sunglasses nearly obliterated the child's face. An allergy to sunlight, no doubt.

"Is that your son?"

Howard looked back at the child, who now came to stand beside him. "Oh no, ma'am. This is Otto Diesewelt. Say, hello, Otto."

Otto offered her a toothless smile but said nothing.

"Lela told me you're the young man who had the first UFO sighting."

Howard beamed as he flashed an arm toward the theme park that surrounded them. "This is all because of me."

She tried to stifle a snigger. "Because of the spaceship you saw."

"All I saw was lights. Are you getting cotton candy, too?"

"What color?"

"I'm getting blue and Otto's getting green."

Before she could explain that she meant the colors of the lights, Howard turned back around in line.

Yes, this was definitely a town full of saucer kooks.

CHAPTER FIVE

Pleasance stepped off the plane and onto a rollable bank of stairs that attendants had pushed up to the doorway. Most of the passengers moved with her on the tarmac toward the terminal entrance with nervous laughs – a far cry from the white knuckles and green complexions they'd suffered during the landing. The dips and shudders of the aircraft stalls during the approach did little to rattle Pleasance. She'd touched down on everything from tiny dirt strips to Himalayan mountain lakes. Just because the runway was a bit short and the pilot had to burn a little rubber to stop was no cause for alarm.

She stepped over a bent child throwing up on the pavement and strode into the building. A sign in large block letters over the entrance read, "Silverville."

A throng of people crowded the baggage claim area, forcing Pleasance to elbow her way up to the conveyor belt. She glanced over the heads of the other new arrivals for any sign of Uncle Perry and Aunt Lela, but she saw no one she recognized.

As luggage appeared on the belt, an older woman struggled to lug an oversized cardboard box to the floor.

"Here, let me help you with that," Pleasance offered.

"Oh, I couldn't possibly ask you –"

But before the woman could finish her sentence, Pleasance hoisted the box onto her shoulder. "Where to?"

"My car is way out in the parking lot."

"No problem. You lead the way."

She followed the shuffling senior citizen out the door and to her vehicle and waited while the woman opened the trunk. Pleasance deposited the box in the car and slammed the lid shut. A block of dried mud fell from the fender and shattered on the cement.

"You live here?" Pleasance asked.

"Yes. I'm back from visiting my daughter for the weekend."

Pleasance looked at a clumpy layer of dirt clinging to the wheel wells. "You live on a ranch or farm?"

The old woman frowned. "Yes, next to that kook, Chantale Getty-Schwartz. The one with the buffalo farm, and –" Without warning, she began to sing:

"BUFFALO GALS, WON'T YOU COME OUT TONIGHT?
COME OUT TONIGHT, COME OUT TONIGHT?"

Her face reddened as she spun and threw her purse into the driver's seat, mumbling "Sorry" over her shoulder. She hopped in the car and gunned it toward the exit.

"What the hell!" Pleasance shrugged and went back into the airport to retrieve her own luggage.

By that time, the crowd had thinned and only a few bags still circled on the conveyor. None of them hers. She walked over to the ticket counter to file a missing luggage claim.

"Can I help you?" a middle-aged man asked her from behind the desk. His crisp white shirt contrasted with the Cargill feed cap perched slightly askew on his head.

"Yes, thank you." Pleasance quickly read his name tag. "My luggage didn't make it, Mr. Montgomery."

"Pat, call me Pat."

"Okay, Pat, should I fill out a form?"

He pulled a piece of paper out from under the counter and handed her a pencil. "If you'll just put down the description of your luggage."

"Yeah, I know this song and dance."

Pat jumped out from behind the counter and danced a little jig while he sang,

"YANKEE DOODLE, KEEP IT UP
YANKEE DOODLE DANDY
MIND THE MUSIC AND THE STEP
AND WITH THE GIRLS BE HANDY."

Pleasance staggered back two steps and dropped the form on the floor.

"Sad, isn't it?" The voice was Perry's.

* * *

Every time Pleasance bent her arms, the elastic on the sleeves of her borrowed muumuu tightened uncomfortably around her biceps. She leaned as far forward as she could to meet her herbal tea half way.

Madame Pompeii held a black cat on her lap as she eyed Pleasance's restrictive movement. "It's the biggest dress I own."

"It's okay, Aunt Penny – I mean, Madame Pompeii." Pleasance inwardly rolled her eyes at her relative's latest identity. "My luggage will show up sooner or later."

Lela walked into the living room carrying a tray of sliced apples and grapes, which she set on the table between Perry and the other two women.

"I'd serve cookies," Lela said, "but, well, you know." She glanced at Perry and Madame Pompeii.

"No, I don't know," Pleasance said. "What's going on around here? Uncle Perry, you said you'd explain why people are acting so strange."

Perry opened his mouth to speak but then closed it and shook his head.

"They're under a curse, Pleasance," Madame Pompeii proclaimed as she stroked her new cat. "Plain and simple as that."

"What?"

"We don't really know," Lela said. With much hesitation, she recapped the events of the past three weeks – how, first, bread began attacking people and how shortly there afterwards, they broke out in song at odd moments.

"It seems to be a progressive thing," she continued. "I haven't sung a song for four days now, so I may be over it."

"'Over it?' You mean like the flu?" Pleasance couldn't hide the incredulous look that must have spread across her face.

"Sort of. The symptoms affect some people more than others, and it certainly seems contagious. And it's starting to affect more people all the time." Lela patted Perry's shoulder. "He'll be singing soon."

"Come on! You can't be serious. This is a joke, right?" Pleasance looked at her Uncle Perry, the man who'd always been the anchor of the Pantiwyckes. The man who had led the last family outing to New Guinea, chewing off leeches as they splashed across jungle streams, the man who had chased down wild boars and killed them with his bare hands, who had tackled cannibals, pinned them in a scissors hold, and forced them to listen to recitations of "The Rime of the Ancient Mariner." And no man alive would have had the guts he'd had to take on three scimitar-carrying Bedouins in Tunisia. Pleasance remembered that day well.

"Pretend you're having a seizure," he'd whispered to her in the desert when the locals had caught him and Pleasance pilfering ancient scrolls from a rock crevice. She'd felt more like peeing her pants but managed to keep her cool and follow his lead.

"A holy sign from Allah!" he'd shouted to the Bedouins as she rolled up her eyes and started to convulse.

When the three attackers paused and came closer, Pleasance cold-cocked one with a flailing fist while Perry subdued the other two.

What a swash-buckling, fearless figure he'd always been. But now he looked unsure how to handle this so-called curse.

"It's no joke," Lela replied. "At least, no one around here is laughing. In fact, you'd be hard pressed to find anyone who's even willing to talk about it."

Pleasance looked from Lela to Perry. She didn't know how to respond. Had Silverville's high altitude affected everyone's thinking? She'd seen examples of mass hysteria before in the jungles of Central America, where people became convinced they were under the spell of a powerful *bruja*. Believing made it a reality. If the witch cursed them with an impending death, the next person who died was because of the *bruja*'s sorcery. But that wasn't magic, just a high mortality rate in a backwoods region with few medical services.

She looked accusingly at Madame Pompeii. "Aunt Penny, did you tell them they were under a curse?"

"I certainly did!" Her aunt seemed to mash the cat into her lap with strokes of guilty energy. "But it didn't take a psychic to figure that one out."

"How come you don't have it?" Pleasance asked.

All eyes turned to Madame Pompeii.

"Yes, why don't you have it?" Lela demanded.

"Me? I'm protected by forces that you couldn't possibly understand."

Perry seemed to rise out of his slump and jump to his feet. "Whoa, whoa, let me think about this for a minute." He paced as he talked. "As far as I know, everyone in our neighborhood has it. Locals I see downtown have it. But now that you mention it, I haven't seen any symptoms in out-of-towners."

"You're right, Perry," Lela exclaimed. "And I haven't seen any signs of it in the visiting church group who've been camping just outside town the past three weeks."

"What's your point?" Pleasance asked.

Perry stopped and faced everyone. "It's just locals. People who really live here. They're the ones with the symptoms!"

Everyone in the living room fell silent. Except the cat, who began a series of growling complaints at her mistress's rough handling.

Madame Pompeii gasped as the cat scratched her wrist. She looped her thumbs under the cat's front legs and raised it to face her. She seemed to talk to the cat as much as to the company around her. "Ptolemy and I are going to take care of it."

From a cage in the corner, an annoying parrot began to squawk, "Chickety, chick! chick, chick!"

"Okaaay," Pleasance said, standing up. "I'm going to the bedroom to make a phone call, and when I come back, you're all going to tell me this is 'let's put one over on Pleasance' day."

She tugged the muumuu out of her butt and walked down the hall to Perry and Lela's bedroom.

* * *

Pleasance flipped open her new cell phone and dialed the number, waiting for the message on the answering machine. But it only took two rings to connect.

"*Hola.*"

"Tomás, is that you?"

"*Sí*, who else? Pleasance, I try to call you but your phone, she's disconnected."

"Yeah, well, that's a long story."

"I got your message, but you leave no number in Colorado."

She gave him her new cell number and asked him how things were going.

"*Bueno* after my hand heals."

"What are you talking about?" On the dresser, Pleasance spotted three old coins and picked one up to get a better look. She held the coin to the light streaming in the window and studied the features of the crowned shield of the House of Hapsburg. She turned the coin over and saw the stamp of the Maltese Cross. Definitely Spanish. Late 1500s during the reign of Phillip II.

"The Three Fools know where you are." He paused. "They force me to tell, or they cut off more fingers."

Pleasance gripped the coin in her fist. "They cut off a finger?"

"Let's just say I count only to *nueve* now."

"Bastards!"

"They might try to follow you. They think you have the mask."

She snorted. What if they knew an eighty-year-old cripple had swiped the mask from right under their noses? "Those idiots don't worry me. They're so stupid they couldn't follow a trail of bread crumbs."

"You be careful anyway."

"Hey, sorry about the finger," she offered.

"I no go bowling now."

"Tomás, Xlohil doesn't have a bowling alley."

"One day it might."

"You take care. Call me if you hear anything."

She snapped the phone shut.

* * *

Pleasance went back into the living room and into the middle of a conversation.

"The key to this whole curse is going to come from my familiar," Madame Pompeii asserted, patting her cat's head.

From the corner, the annoying parrot began to squawk again. "Key to the curse! Key to the curse!"

Madame Pompeii whipped her head in the bird's direction. "Pandora, shut up, you idiot!"

Proust trotted over to the parrot cage and stared, hackles raised. Everyone watched as the dog's line of sight tracked along the ceiling from Pandora to the other end of the room and back again.

Pleasance, still standing in the doorway, moved over to Lela to show what she'd plucked off the dresser. "Is this one of the coins you found, Aunt Lela?"

"Yes." Lela appeared relieved at the change of subject. "Do you think it's an old Spanish coin?"

Pleasance nodded. "Definitely Conquistador era."

"Are they valuable?"

The coins were in poor condition, the edges worn smooth and the impressions almost unreadable. "Well, they might be worth ten to twenty bucks a piece. They're pretty beat up."

Lela's face fell at the news, and Pleasance quickly added, "But didn't you say there were other artifacts found a long time ago around here? There still could be something out there worth looking for."

Perry exhaled. "The problem is that Lela doesn't remember exactly where she found them."

"But Grady might know," Lela said. "He's the rancher I told you about. He might be able to point us in the general direction."

Might? Valuable Spanish treasure and someone just "might" be able to help? Pleasance had traveled over two-thousand miles on the chance that she could cash in on whatever an old geezer had left in a pasture fifty years ago. What would she say to Winchester – that the people in this town *might* know where maybe half a million dollars worth of artifacts lay buried?

"Do you suppose we should call and ask him?" Pleasance asked.

"Why yes, that's a good idea. I'll phone him right now."

At that moment the doorbell rang, and Perry rose to answer it. "It's for you, Pleasance," he shouted from the foyer. "It's your luggage."

Her uncle, accompanied by a teenager dressed in khaki shirt and jeans, walked in and set two suitcases on the living room floor.

"Thanks!" Pleasance automatically reached into her empty muumuu pocket searching for tip money.

"I'll get it," Perry offered, and handed the kid a five-dollar bill. "Will this do ya?"

The delivery boy replied:

*"THE CAMPTOWN LADIES SING THIS SONG,
DOO-DA, DOO-DA.
THE CAMPTOWN RACETRACK'S FIVE MILES LONG
OH, DE DOO-DA DAY."*

Perry closed the door on the song trailing after the delivery boy. "That's me in a few days," he said with a grim face. Pleasance had no chance to respond because Lela announced, "I just talked to Grady and he said he might remember where he found those artifacts."

Pleasance sighed. "That's good, Aunt Lela." She grabbed the suitcases and started across the room. She couldn't wait to shed the muumuu.

"But that's not all he said."

Pleasance turned to look at her.

"He also said he knows why all this strange stuff is happening."

* * *

Pleasance hopped out of the car and waited for her relatives to follow. A gray-muzzled ranch dog trotted up and focused on her with its one good eye. She reached down to pet the mutt, but it skirted away from her hand and skulked over to pee on Perry's tire.

She looked around. The scene was just what she expected. Toward the ranch house, marigolds and tulips flourished in an immaculate flower garden; sheets and blankets waved gently on a clothes line. Beside a dilapidated barn stood a corral where an ancient-looking red horse glared at them with flattened ears. A giant cottonwood tree with a rope dangling from one branch shaded a small cabin at the far end of the driveway.

"Oh, Grady must have company," Lela said, pointing at a late model Toyota SUV parked at the cabin.

The SUV seemed a stark contrast to the beat-up pickup truck and a '78 Oldsmobile sedan sitting in front of the main house.

The side door squeaked open and out stepped a character straight from a Charles Russell painting, only the colors weren't as vivid and the canvas looked a little cracked.

"Afternoon, Grady," Perry called to the figure as they walked to the porch.

Grady motioned them inside and turned back through the door ahead of them.

Lela placed her hands on Madame Pompeii's and Pleasance's shoulders to slow them down. "Let me do most of the talking. Grady doesn't think much of strangers."

Pleasance nodded.

"And Madame Pompeii," Lela continued," you might want to slip that pendant in your pocket."

Madame Pompeii clutched a feathered spiderweb necklace that hung from her neck. "My Dream-Catcher?"

"Hm, and ditch the star pasted to your forehead."

The psychic started to object, but Pleasance reached across Lela and ripped off the star. Delicate negotiations with suspicious locals. This was familiar territory.

The homey aroma of a freshly baked pie met them as they stepped through the mud room and into the kitchen. They crossed over well-worn, creaky linoleum to a table where Perry and Grady already sat.

Just as they pulled out the remaining empty chairs, a skeletal woman entered from the hallway.

"Land alive! I didn't know you folks were here yet." She lifted a net off her head, her salt and pepper hair never changing shape.

"Thanks, Leona," Lela said, "for letting us come over on such short notice."

Leona set a steaming rhubarb pie on the middle of the table. "Why, we just love having company, don't we, Grady?"

From where Pleasance sat, she could see Leona press and hold a fork against Grady's elbow until he said, "Yep." She pulled the fork away and smiled at her visitors.

"Pie?" Leona asked.

* * *

"So all this weird stuff happened to you, too?" Perry asked.

Grady took a swig from his coffee cup, apparently dry in the throat. It was probably more talking than the old rancher was used to. Pleasance had kept quiet the whole time Grady told his tale about finding Spanish artifacts and bringing the coins home as a kid.

She was still having trouble buying any of this. During the course of her career, she had pilfered cursed tombs, withstood the hexes of local shamans, and walked under countless excavation ladders with never a shade of bad luck. Still, superstition was sometimes a useful card to play. She asked Grady, "And you think returning the coins ended the strange behavior?"

Grady nodded. "Yep, didn't want nothing to do with that stuff no more."

"What about the other artifacts – were they still there?"

"Didn't take no time to notice. I high-tailed it out of there quick as I could."

Lela's pie fork stopped midway between her plate and her mouth. "Wait a minute. I'd heard you couldn't remember where you found those artifacts."

"Just left out that part of the story. People kept asking about the helmet and sword."

Perry asked, "You lied?"

Grady twisted the cup in his hand, studying the chipped enamel along the rim. "Didn't need all those folks traipsing around our pasture. Or the same shenanigans happening to our neighbors."

"But you do know," Pleasance pushed, "where the site is."

"Yes, ma'am."

"Would you be willing to show me?

"Nope."

Pleasance hoped the smile she returned wasn't too brittle. She was going to need a different tack to pry out the information. "But my Aunt Lela – she'll also need to get rid of the coins."

"Didn't say I wouldn't help." He turned to Lela. "You bring those by, and I'll take care of them."

Lela agreed and set her napkin on the table. Grady pushed back his chair and stood up. At almost the same time, Leona started to collect the empty pie plates.

"But aren't you afraid to touch the coins?" Pleasance asked, following him through the mud room.

"Ain't gonna. Got somebody else to do it." Grady picked up his hat from a peg and set it on his head. He held the door open and waited for everybody to leave.

Pleasance hung back. She still had to figure out a way to get to the site.

"Listen, Mr. O'Grady," she said close to his ear, "how would you like a new pickup truck? "

He didn't answer.

She continued, "I've got someone who'll pay real money to find out where that site is."

For several seconds, he said nothing. He tugged at his brim. "Afternoon, ma'am."

He closed the door in her face.

* * *

Grady walked back into the kitchen.

Leona was washing the dishes. "You should have told them the third thing that happened when you had those coins."

"Didn't see it was necessary since Lela is getting rid of them."

* * *

A liver-spotted hand pulled open the curtains in the guest cabin. The old man fingered a Pez in his palm. He smiled as he watched Pleasance and her party drive away. This would require that he more closely scrutinize her activities henceforth.

57

CHAPTER SIX

Lela didn't remember Madame Pompeii as the one who discovered the source of the curse – although her unwelcome in-law insisted on taking credit for it.

"Aren't you glad I channeled your thoughts into calling Grady?" Madame Pompeii asked as Perry's car rolled into the outskirts of town. "I always knew that if I could find the curse, I could save the town."

Like hell, Lela thought. The old charlatan hadn't even paid attention while the rest of the family tried to make sense of everything. She just crooned New-Age babble to that hateful black cat, which spent most of its time terrorizing Proust.

Within a few minutes, Alien Landing theme park came into view. So many people crowded around the entrance that the vehicle had to slow to avoid hitting anyone. On the edge stood Howard Beacon, holding the hand of a child who wore a hooded sweatshirt pulled over his head.

"Who is Howard with?" Lela asked. "And why is he dressed like that? It must be eighty-five degrees."

From the backseat, Madame Pompeii said, "That's his friend, Otto."

Lela swiveled in her seat in time to see her sister-in-law leaning in the direction of the rearview mirror to reattach the star to the middle of her forehead.

"The kid's got a sun allergy," Madame Pompeii explained. "At least that's what I got from his aura."

Perry stopped at the crosswalk while a family of four, wearing alien antenna headbands, marched across the road single file.

"Such nonsense." Madame Pompeii clucked her tongue and made a face. "The only things of any value inside those gates are the psychic booths."

Lela studied the alien motifs adorning the fence surrounding the theme park as if she were seeing them for the first time. Madame Pompeii was right: They were nonsense. The town deserved a more dignified attraction, something that reflected local values. Something that made sense.

"I agree," Lela said. "This is ridiculous. We'd have been better off erecting a monument to … to chickens!"

Lela clasped her hand to her mouth. She couldn't believe what she'd just suggested. What was worse, she meant it. Chickens. They were fine animals who never started wars. And they ate bugs. They came in a variety of dazzling colors and they took good care of their eggs. *Oh my God! How many eggs have I eaten? How many chicks never got to play in the sunlight or peck at gravel because of me?*

"Aunt Lela?" Pleasance and everyone else in the car stared at her. "There's nothing wrong with eating eggs."

Heat rose into Lela's cheeks. "I was talking out loud?"

Perry reached over to pat Lela's hand. "It's been a long day. This coin business is really getting to you. Let's all go get some supper. Is everyone up for Bill's BBQ?"

"Fine, fine," Lela snapped. "Just no hot wings!"

* * *

Maurice surveyed the row of tidily arranged ascots that filled the upper compartment of his suitcase. He selected one with just a blush of apricot to match his socks. He chuckled at his propitious talent to once again outmaneuver Pleasance. How careless of her to repeat Grady's name over the phone that fateful day he overheard her conversation. Poor child. Had she learned nothing from his example? By the time he had arranged to travel to Silverville, he already had Mr. O'Grady's phone number and address in his pocket.

He adjusted the ascot, tucking it neatly inside his collar and around his papery throat. He sat on the bed and reached over to snap the garters to his socks. During his initial phone contact, the rancher hung up on him as soon as Maurice mentioned the term, "Spanish artifact." Maurice had immediately redialed and inquired again. This time, silence on the other end.

Finally, the rancher spoke. "How'd you know about them things?"

Maurice laughed. "I have friends all over the world. Perhaps some even in Silverville. I would like to purchase these artifacts from you, Mr. O'Grady."

"You mean you want to take them?"

"Well, yes. Buy them and take them."

More silence, but then Mr. O'Grady said, "How far away?"

Oddly, the man seemed more concerned with where the artifacts were going rather than how much he would receive in remuneration. In the end, the rancher refused any money at all but agreed to the transaction only if the artifacts would leave the state.

Most baffling. Who knew how the minds of rustic denizens worked?

Maurice opened the door to the guest cabin and gripped the handles of his walker to begin the journey to the main house. Knowing full well that someone might be watching, he took slow, deliberate steps as he negotiated the rough-graded road that connected the two buildings, side-stepping various piles of excrement left by unidentified animals. As he approached the house, that unattractive cur circled behind him with suspicion. The dog would first appear on one side and then the other, but always close to Maurice's heels.

"Yes, yes, my good fellow. No need to hurry me along."

When he felt a tug at his pant leg, he paused and surveyed the windows of the ranch house but saw no one. He extracted a palm-sized taser from his pocket, leaving a stunned dog on the ground behind him.

* * *

"What's wrong with Rex?" Leona said as she handed Grady a wrench. "I just saw him fall over."

Grady, on hands and knees, whacked at a loose pipe under the sink. "What're you talking about?"

"Rex, he just fell over walking behind Mr. LeVieux."

"Probably that new dog food." Grady grabbed the edge of the counter and pulled himself upright. Through the rippled window pane, the figure of their guest made a slow approach toward the house, not seeming to notice the prostrate dog.

Grady smacked his lips once. Two sets of house-callers in one afternoon were two too many, and the rancher was beginning to regret letting the foreigner stay in the bunk house. 'Course, it did make it easier to keep an eye on him since they'd made their deal. If Grady hadn't seen the peculiar goings-on in town, he'd never have agreed to let the Easterner set a foot on the premises. Cantankerous bread and sudden singing were all too familiar – even if they had happened to Grady more than fifty years ago.

As a youngster, he'd talked his dad into letting him go on the last wild-horse roundup in the Valley. They'd put him on Old Red, not much more than a mustang himself, and before the day was over, Grady found himself eating dirt while his mount raced home without him.

On the way back, his boot kicked up a couple of coins tangled in sagebrush roots. They were old, really old, and he pocketed them. As he stood up, he saw a cave on the arroyo wall, and he walked over to look inside. The first thing that caught his attention was the helmet, flared out on the sides, still shining despite its obvious old age. Beside it lay a sleek metal sword, its handle crusted with colored stones. All at once he noticed the jawbone. But it weren't no animal. Grady bolted from the cave and hightailed it back to the horse camp.

When he showed his coins to the men in the camp and told them what else he'd found, they all laughed and told him he'd been in the sun too long.

It took a couple of days for the bread to start misbehaving. Grady began to get nervous every time his mama pulled out her baking pans. To his horror, the bread started flying at her, too, but she blamed him for throwing biscuits. A couple days more and they were taking him to the woodshed for singing during church services, which may not have been a problem except that it was a song he learned behind the schoolhouse about a man from Nantucket. Pretty soon, he wasn't the only one in town singing "out of tune" at the services.

The last straw came when his mother asked him to go to the coop and wring a chicken's neck for supper. Grady couldn't get himself to do it even though he'd killed hens dozens of times before. Tears streaming down his face, he opened the coop door and chased all the chickens out. "You're free! You're free!" he shouted, waving his arms to shoo them into the hills. It got him a licking he wouldn't soon forget, and that's when he put two and two together. He'd never gotten into trouble until he'd found those coins.

Early the next morning, Grady had tiptoed from the house and headed back to the cave. He'd thrown all the artifacts he'd found into a pool inside the cave, including the coins he'd kept in his pocket. After that day, the bread stayed in the pans, church services went uninterrupted, and chicken shit smelled just as bad as it used to.

No one ever suspected the cause of all that trouble, and he never told anyone about the curse until he met Leona years later. His story about the find, however, had floated around town so long it had become local legend.

When the knock sounded through the mudroom, Leona went to open the door and invited in their guest into the adjoining kitchen.

"Afternoon, Mr. LeVieux," Grady said, pulling out a chair only for himself. "What can I do you for?"

Mr. LeVieux bowed with great flourish and shuffled over to an empty chair. "In preparation for our little expedition tomorrow, would you be so kind as to recommend appropriate foot apparel?"

"Ain't gonna be tomorrow." Grady pointed toward the hills several miles from the window above the sink. "See them black clouds out there? Been raining for the last couple days, and more on the way."

"Do you mean to suggest some delay?"

"Reckon so. No way the pickup will get up there 'til things dry out."

"But Mr. O'Grady –"

"Ain't no use even trying."

Mr. Le Vieux drummed the table twice with his fingers, stopped and exhaled. "Of course, you would know better than I what's feasible in this semi-arid landscape."

Grady waited for the man to get up and leave, but he didn't.

"Oh!" Leona said. "Would you like some coffee?"

"You wouldn't by chance happen to have on hand a spot of Earl Grey tea?"

"Uh, I have Lipton. Would that do?"

"A splendid alternative. Perhaps with a slight dusting of cinnamon?"

Grady saw her shoot a quick glance at him, and he knew damn well it was intended to keep his mouth shut. "I can manage that," she said.

While Leona busied herself with the Lipton, their guest brushed dog hair off his pant cuff and turned to Grady. "Please, Mr. O'Grady, shall we dispense with inane formalities and refer to each other by our surnames? You may call me Maurice. And may I call you…"

"Mr. O'Grady works just fine."

Grady kept his eyes zeroed in on the fancy fart's face, but he never saw the response he expected.

"Excellent, Mr. O'Grady."

Grady twisted uncomfortably in his seat. "Leona, where's that tea?"

"By the way, I couldn't help but notice your earlier callers. Did I, by chance, happen to recognize my dear friend, Pleasance Pantiwycke?"

"You mean that big, pushy gal?"

Maurice seemed to laugh with affection. "The very one."

"She wanted to know about the treasure in the cave, too."

Tarnation, how many folks were after those things anyway? Didn't matter. Maurice had made the deal first.

"I hope it's not necessary to remind you, Mr. O'Grady, that we have a gentlemen's agreement concerning these artifacts."

"I know that. A deal's a deal."

"Then can I assume…"

"She don't know nothing more than anybody else."

Maurice steepled his hands and relaxed into the chair. "Excellent."

"Just one more thing though," Grady said. "You gotta take some coins, too, when I get them from Lela."

Leona set the fresh-brewed tea before Maurice.

"Coins?" the old cripple asked. "You mean there's more?"

Damn right, there's more. In Grady's mind, there were two ways to handle the curse. He could either return the coins to the cave after Lela handed them over, or better, pawn them and everything else off on Maurice and get the whole bundle out of town. Because some day, another local was going to find that stuff, and it would start all over again.

"Hurry up and drink that tea," Grady said. "We got chores to do."

* * *

"I've offered just about as much generosity as I care to."

The voice sounded brittle on the phone, and Pleasance remembered the ominous threat in the little story about the trade. She said, "This is a sure shot, Mr. Winchester. Give me just a few more days."

No response. Then she heard a deep breath. The words that followed sounded like they hissed through clenched teeth. "One week, Pleasance. I've been financing you for the past few months, with nothing to show for my investment. *Nada.*"

"Okay, okay, I know we've had a run of bad luck, but –"

"One week. You have one week to deliver the acquisitions, or you're going to owe me –"

"I'm doing my best to –"

"One week. Goodbye, Pleasance." And he hung up.

The plastic of the cordless phone she held cracked before she could relax her grip. Shit. Since she'd last landed anything of value for him, Winchester had financed her trip to Mexico – not a particularly cheap expedition. Roundtrip plane fare, hotel, car rental, Tomás's fee. Then she'd talked him into advancing her money for the trip to Silverville. She made a quick mental calculation and figured he'd probably spent close to ten thousand dollars. But this time with nothing to show.

But wasn't she doing everything she could? It wasn't her fault that old fart Grady was so uncooperative. She just needed time to figure out a way around the rancher. For the Silverville deal, she'd only asked Winchester for enough money to last a few days, and now that was gone. She dared not ask for more.

"Why are you looking so glum?" Uncle Perry asked, walking into the kitchen. Without warning, he put his hand over his heart and began to expand his lungs.

Before he could open his mouth in a burst of musical Tourette's, Pleasance clutched his shoulders and shook him. "Richard Nixon was a drag queen!"

It worked; he seemed too stunned to sing. "What?"

"Nothing." She backed him up to a chair and pressed on his shoulders until he sat down. "So, did you get the coins back to Grady?"

"Yessiree. Brought them over this morning."

Pleasance sat across from him, propping two muscular forearms on the table. "And?"

"And what? Oh yeah, the coins. It wasn't as easy as just handing them over. Grady wouldn't touch them. He tossed a saddle bag out the front door and hollered through the screen to leave the coins in the bag on the porch step. What a cracked nut."

Uncle Perry just figured that out? Pleasance sighed. The saddle bag incident was beside the point. She needed to know when to start her surveillance on Grady's movements.

"Did he say when he planned to take the coins back?"

"Won't be anytime soon. It's raining too hard, and he said he'd never get his truck up there. Also, there's an underwater aquifer that's probably flooding the cave. Might have to wait another week."

Another week. Winchester wouldn't wait that long. He didn't with Cappelli, her predecessor. When her former lover failed to cough up the goods Winchester had paid him to get, Cappelli had disappeared. Until she'd started working for Winchester, she'd always had been able to fulfill her contracts. Maybe she was out of her league after all.

She had to get her hands on the treasure pronto. But in the meantime, she needed enough money to bridge the gap. It wasn't like she could "borrow" and hock the jet skis in the garage for a couple of weeks, or start an under-the-radar betting operation – Silverville was too small for that, and word was bound to get back to Uncle Perry. She'd never do anything to embarrass him in his home town. No, quick money was going to be a problem unless . . . Pleasance could hardly bring herself to think the unthinkable. She was going to have to get a real job.

"Uncle Perry, do you know where I could get a job?"

"What do you mean? Don't you already work for a museum?"

"Yes – no, uh, well ... all the art historians are on strike. Orders from the union."

Perry bit his lower lip and tilted his head sideways. "Art historians have a union?"

Pleasance had no idea, but she was on a roll. "Of course. And we're striking because, because ... the museum banned us from eating pizza at lunch."

"Huh?"

"They say garlic breath is bad for the paintings," she said, trying to sound perturbed.

Perry nodded as though he appreciated her dilemma.

"So, I need to find a short-term job until this blows over." She never gave him a chance to think through her explanation, and added, "Any ideas?"

"You don't need a job as long as you're staying with us. Besides, there aren't many options around here."

"I'm not mooching off of family, Uncle Perry. Surely there's something."

Leaning back in the chair, he tapped his cheek for a moment. "Well, there's the movie company. Someone at the golf course told me that they're looking for local crew members."

She liked the sound of that. She was spending too much time waiting around for Grady anyway.

At that moment, a two-by-four plank of wood bobbed past the kitchen window.

"And there's some sort of new telemarketing company that just came to town. I bet they're hiring."

Pleasance stood up and peered through the window. "What's Aunt Lela doing in the yard?"

"Oh, she's building a chicken coop."

Lela had assembled a stack of boards and several rolls of chicken wire in the corner of the yard. At the hips of her bib overalls, a tool belt jiggled with a hammer, carpenter's square, and pliers.

Pleasance frowned. "Shouldn't we stop her?"

"Oh, I don't know. It keeps her occupied."

* * *

Lela filed into Silverville's town meeting hall along with other locals, relieved that she could attend as a concerned community member. She no longer had the responsibility to preside over the gathering as mayor. In fact, she took advantage of her diminished role by sitting near the back.

The rows of chairs arranged before her began to fill as she squeezed her hands together. She winced at the blisters on her right forefinger and thumb from pounding nails on her chicken coop. Thunder and the sound of rain reverberated through the town hall each time someone opened the doors, stomping boots, some shaking out umbrellas, a few shaking out wet chickens. The murmurs of townsfolk mixed with an undercurrent of clucks from leashed fowl.

A well-dressed woman sat down on the chair next to Lela, a chicken in tow sporting a rhinestone harness. The woman picked up the bird and placed it on her lap.

Lela leaned over and whispered, "That's a beautiful Leghorn."

The woman smiled and glowed.

Mayor Earl Bob Jackson called the meeting to order. Once Silverville's UFO expert, he'd moved up the ranks to become indispensable to town government. Lela could see his new wife, Skippy, sitting a few rows ahead of her.

The strike of the mayor's gavel silenced the crowd but startled the chickens into a cacophony of complaining clucks.

"Order! Order!" shouted Carl, the town's sheriff. "If you can't control your – your pets, I'll have to clear them from the meeting!"

Indignant gasps and objections rose from the crowd. Lela couldn't understand this lack of sympathy for the majestic birds.

Someone stood and began singing verses of "Old MacDonald's Farm."

"Gag that person!" Carl commanded. Several people jumped on the crooner and shoved a stocking cap in his mouth.

After the din died down, the mayor spoke. "The first – or rather, the only – order of business today is to consider why this odd wave of occurrences is happening to our community, and how to address it."

People in the gathering nodded to each other, and finally a woman's voice suggested it might be the water.

"I guess it could be," Earl Bob said. "But hasn't Silverville been using the same source for the past seventy-five years?"

"Maybe it's contaminated," said someone from the front row. "I bet the aliens are using Silverville as an experimental lab. They dumped something into our water."

"To keep us under control when they take us up to the mother ship to probe our anuses." It was the local hardware store owner, who'd lived in Silverville all his life.

"I don't think that's it at all," said airport employee Pat Montgomery. "If the aliens did contaminate our water, it was only to open our eyes to another significant species on this planet." He clutched his Rhode Island Red closer to his breast.

Dissention divided the crowd into two camps, one arguing the quality of water and the other arguing the quality of chickens.

The county's public utilities supervisor stood. "It's not the water! We have it tested regularly. And there's been no additives since Howard saw that UFO."

A fat man raised his hand.

Lela groaned to herself. Why couldn't that overbearing crackpot, Buford Price, ever keep his mouth shut?

Buford cleared his throat. "I don't have these problems."

"Not yet!" shouted someone from the crowd.

"Like I was saying before ..." Buford scowled at the man who interrupted him, and continued, "I don't have these problems, but I think I know why some of us do."

The mayor asked, "And what would that be?"

"I'm thinking the aliens that came here two years ago implanted something in the necks of weaker-minded townspeople."

The hall erupted with simultaneous mass objections: "Asshole!" – "Pompous idiot!" – "Loser!"

The mayor's gavel rapped the table until everyone settled down enough to let Buford continue. "Hell, it could even be interference from other dimensions. Like an inter-dimensional traveler playing with our minds. Everyone knows that Silverville sits on ley lines. That can cause all kinds of weird stuff."

"Sit down, Buford, and shut up!" Lela called out. Buford obediently plopped his backside into the seat. She slapped a hand over her mouth, mortified at what she'd just done. An old habit – her usual response to Buford when she was mayor.

Earl Bob said, "It's clear we have a problem, regardless of the cause. We have to come up with some solutions before the national media gets a hold of this. We don't want a repeat of two years ago."

Lela shuddered. When word first got out about the possible alien sighting, Buford Price turned the community into a sideshow attraction with his theme park and museum. Newspaper and television reporters had swarmed the streets. Tourists and truth seekers soon followed, changing the flavor of their little town. True, the economy had soared, but the consequences had been overpriced housing, higher local taxes, and a main street dominated by UFO curio shops.

Montgomery, still caressing his bird, complained, "I think we have a bigger problem. There's a new fast-food restaurant in town that sells broasted chicken."

"And what about the fried chicken place!" someone else yelled out.

A third person shouted, "We need to shut these restaurants down!"

Earl Bob closed his eyes and shook his head. "Again, I want to steer us toward a solution for the *larger* problem at hand. It may be time for us to think about calling in the Center for Disease Control before it spreads to all of us."

"The only disease we've got in this town," Montgomery continued, "is that stupid theme park of Buford's. I move we change Alien Landing to Fowl Fantasia, and make it a sanctuary for our feathered friends." He stroked the plumage of the squirming bird clamped in his arms.

Immediately, nine attendees seconded the motion.

Carl bent over and whispered to Earl Bob, who nodded. Then the sheriff walked over to look out the window. He jumped with surprise, exclaiming, "Oh my God, someone's burning chickens down the street!"

A third of the chairs overturned as chicken advocates scrambled toward the door, Lela among them. Short and not particularly spry, she found herself jostled to the back of the stampede. Just as she managed to squeeze out the door, she heard Earl Bob say, "Quick, lock them out!"

Outside the building, chicken owners fled down the street. Some dragged their complaining pets by leash, others trying to tuck them under raincoats amid a flurry of feathers and squawks. Lela looked after them but saw no sign of chicken-burning zealots. She walked back to the door and pressed her ear against the solid oak. Murmurs were all she could make out. Then she remembered the key at the bottom of her purse, issued to her when she served as mayor. She'd always meant to return it, but she was glad to have it now. Going around the corner of the building, she looked to see if anyone was watching, slipped a hand into her purse to retrieve the key, and opened the back door.

She followed the hall that led to a dropped curtain situated behind the meeting dais. Pushing the fabric aside just an inch or two, she could see the backs of Earl Bob and the other City Council members. She could only make out a small slice of the meeting attendees.

"I think it's a mistake to invite the CDC here," Buford was saying. "What kind of publicity would that be for the town?"

"We've got to do *something* before the rest of us get it." Carl's voice filled the meeting hall.

No one offered to speak for several moments, and finally Earl Bob said, "I'm not so sure we're all going to get it." His head turned from side to side, apparently surveying the crowd. "Is there anyone left in here born in Silverville?"

Lela heard no responses.

"I didn't think so," Earl Bob continued. "I don't really know what's going on here, but it seems to me that born-and-bred natives are the ones coming down with all these afflictions."

"My neighbor, Dexter Johnson, got it. He wasn't born here," the new yoga teacher said from a Lotus Position on the floor. "Come to think of it, I never heard this guy sing; he seemed to go straight from the bread to the chicken phase."

"Yeah, my deputy's wife isn't from here, and she just got a few of the symptoms, too," Carl said. "And then she was fine."

"But aren't they both married to natives?" Earl Bob asked.

The people Lela could see appeared to mull this over for a moment. Then the mayor suggested, "Is it possible that true locals get all the symptoms, and people married to locals get a shorter version?"

Earl Bob paused, possibly to let this sink in. "I bet not one person in this room is married to a native or you'd be having symptoms, too." No one contradicted him. "Seems to me this is what it boils down to: We're seeing three different kinds of behavior in the natives. It starts with the bread. That passes, and next comes the singing, followed by the chicken mania. On the other hand, people simply married to natives exhibit partial symptoms."

"Nice guess, *Mr.* Mayor," Buford said, a sneer spreading across his face. "But that's all it is, a guess."

Lela dug a fingernail into one of her blisters to keep from shouting, *Sit down and shut up, Buford!* He'd never been cordial to Earl Bob, and he'd become even worse since Skippy divorced him and married the new mayor.

Chair legs skidded on the floor, and Lela heard heavy footsteps stomping to the edge of the dais as Carl came into view. The sheriff planted his six-foot-plus frame in front of the table and pointed a finger where the remaining audience must be sitting. "Quit being such an asshole, Buford, and let the man talk. We're trying to think through this."

Earl Bob resumed, "Regardless of who has what, I still think the CDC is probably our best solution. What do you think, Carl?"

"Gee, I don't know about that. Maybe we don't need that kind of attention. We don't know if that would kill our tourism or just bring more kooks to town."

Lela leaned so hard into the curtains that she stumbled forward, grasping a fold to regain her balance.

"Hey, I just saw that curtain move!" Buford shouted. "There's somebody back there!"

Before she could turn and run, she heard Carl say, "That's ridiculous. Shut up, Buford, and sit down!"

She could have kissed the sheriff.

The voice of Bob Hardin, a local hot air balloon operator, echoed from the far side of the room. "We could take care of this problem ourselves."

"How?" Earl Bob asked.

"Just take these folks and contain them until they get over it."

Carl spoke up. "You mean like arrest them? I don't have room in my jail for that."

"No, we just escort them off the street when they make a scene and house them in the school gymnasium. School's still out for another month."

Approving murmurs rose from the other council members and the remaining crowd.

Still standing, the sheriff shook his head. "But I don't want those chickens in my squad car. Bob, you've got a van for your balloon. We'll use that."

"Wait a minute," Hardin objected. "I didn't mean –"

Earl Bob rapped his gavel once and announced, "Let's put it to a vote. All those in favor of intercepting afflicted residents with Bob's van and taking them to the school gymnasium, say aye."

CHAPTER SEVEN

Madame Pompeii sat on the couch, hunched over the coffee table, scouring her new crystal ball with window cleaner. Something had to be wrong with it. The first time she'd used it on the previous day, she'd gotten disappointing results. Lela, her first test subject, had seemed resistant to the ball's oracular power. And maybe that was the problem.

Madame Pompeii had dimmed the lights, preparing herself for the session with a soothing cup of chamomile tea, a half hour of meditation, and a consultation with her feline familiar, Ptolemy. Yet the ball revealed something very strange that confused her and only amused Lela. The psychic had been ecstatic when a foggy face began to materialize inside the ball. Features resolved into an older man with receding gray hair and a double chin. Anger radiated from his eyes, tinged with indignation and reproach.

"Look! Look, Lela. There's a face in the ball!"

"Where?"

Both women lurched forward to get a closer look into the crystal, their foreheads colliding and knocking off the star pasted to Madame Pompeii's forehead.

"That's your face reflected," Lela said, rubbing the skin above her eye.

"It's not – unless I'm a sixty-year-old guy with gray hair."

"Well, I don't see anything."

Madame Pompeii had caressed the ball and refocused on the image deep inside the oracular globe. She nearly fell off the couch when the face's mouth began to move, and faint words resonated in her mind.

She crooned to the crystal, "Speak to me, departed one."

Lela had laughed and started to walk away when Madame Pompeii began relating the apparition's words.

"That's ridiculous," Lela said. "It can't be Earl Bob. For one thing, Earl Bob Jackson is younger than that. And for another, he wasn't murdered on any mountain pass. I see him in town all the time."

"Oh. Are you sure?" The seer had felt deflated. Perhaps the head bump had interfered with her power to interpret the ball.

Today, things would be different.

Pleasance strode into the living room with an umbrella and headed for the front door.

"Come here, Pleasance. I'm going to read your future."

"Oh, could it wait? I'm going for a job interview."

"This shouldn't take that long. Besides, it's pouring outside." Madame Pompeii got up and led her new subject toward the couch. "You don't want to arrive at the interview looking drenched."

Pleasance sighed and dropped her umbrella by the table. "Okay, but just for a few minutes."

Madame Pompeii waved her hands in a circular motion over the crystal ball, invoking the assistance of any spirits who might happen to be listening. "Come to us, oh wanderers on the Far Side. We wish to know what the future holds for this young woman."

Nothing happened.

Pleasance fidgeted. "I really need to get to that interview."

"No, no. Just wait."

From the cage against the wall, her parrot, Pandora, began to screech.

"Shut up, you bag of feathers!" the seer scolded.

"Maybe another time, Aunt Penny."

"Wait, wait! I see something!"

From the depths of the crystal ball, three figures began to take shape. They seemed unaware of Madame Pompeii's presence even after repeated entreaties to respond to her. They did, however, seem to know each other because of the way they interacted. The first man tried to slap the second, who ducked, leaving the third man to take the brunt of the blow. Hard to tell if any of this was play or violence. She squinted at the ball for a better look and noticed that all three had dark hair and olive skin.

"Ah, you're about to have an Italian lover, maybe even three."

"Okay, that's great. Gotta run."

When Pleasance started to rise from the couch, Madame Pompeii grabbed her arm and pulled her back down. "Do you know any Italian men?"

Pleasance looked stunned. She stammered, "Uh, there's a guy in New York who sells pretzels."

"Maybe that's the first lover."

Pleasance shook her head. "Don't think so. He's old." She pursed her lips and added, "I used to know another guy who was Italian, but that's over."

"There you have it." The ball did work. "You're about to embark on a torrid Latin love affair. Think of it, Pleasance – Rome, Venice, Florence."

Pandora began to pace back and forth the length of her perch, bobbing her head and flapping her wings. The bird launched to the side of its cage, startling both women, and pressing an eye between the wires to glare at them.

Pleasance returned the glare. "What's wrong with Pandora?"

"Nothing. That stupid bird has a brain the size of a peanut."

But she soon forgot the distraction of the parrot when a new form filled the convex glass. Nothing more than the silhouette of a man surrounded by a swirling haze that exploded with glitter. Fog? No, too bright. Geometric patterns popped in and out of view. The outline of the figure sometimes melded with the haze, sometimes took on definite shape. There seemed something almost sinister in what she saw. Unsettling. The instruction manual never mentioned anything like this.

Was the ball's message for her or for Pleasance? If it was her own, she'd need the protection of specific spells to guard against such possible malevolence. Perhaps a poultice of woodpecker poop, baker's yeast, and dark German beer – was that it? Or maybe a brew of mouthwash and mayonnaise to ward away demons and, of course, gingivitis. If the message targeted Pleasance …

A large hand blocked the vision in the ball. Pleasance was trying to get her attention.

Well, she was a big girl. She could take care of herself. Even so, Madame Pompeii felt compelled to broach the subject.

She turned away from the ball. "You're not involved in any cultish religious groups or black magic, are you?"

The young woman laughed and snorted. "If I was involved in black magic, I'd conjure up some money. As far as religion goes, the only time I've been in a church was to steal – uh, I mean, make a deal for old Romanian relics."

Pleasance waved and walked out the door, leaving Madame Pompeii alone with the disquieting image in the ball.

A rapid pound of footsteps erupted from the hall, coming her way. Proust streaked into the living room, Ptolemy right behind and closing. The pug scooted under the psychic's legs as the cat dropped to its stomach and growled only inches away.

Scooping up her familiar, Madame Pompeii thrust the cat's face toward the crystal. "You know the answer, don't you, my all-seeing friend?"

Together they looked, but this time the creature inside the ball stretched and threaded itself through a black pinpoint. A flash disrupted the scene, and the dark dot reappeared to yawn and spew out gelatinous strings that frothed and thickened into four limbs and a head.

"Hello? Anyone in there who can tell me what's going on?"

Almost unrecognizable human features began to resolve into a visage that stared directly at her. At the same time, intensifying laughter rumbled and vibrated the crystal ball.

Yeowwww! the cat screeched, springing from her hands and darting under her legs. Proust broke into a mournful howl, now trapped between the cat and two beefy human calves. Struggling to rise from the couch, Madame Pompeii slipped in a yellow puddle beneath her feet.

She scolded the cat and the dog, though not entirely sure they were to blame. Retrieving a dishtowel from the kitchen, she swabbed the floor, glancing sideways at the crystal ball. The disturbing image had disappeared.

"Oh, I'm so relieved," she said aloud, dabbing the beads of perspiration on her forehead with the same towel.

She resettled on the couch to pack up the ball, but the three Latin lovers had returned.

She took deep breaths and watched their puzzling antics. From the birdcage, Pandora began to squawk, "*¡Qué mujer más grande! ¡Qué mujer más grande!*"

"Shut up!" Madame Pompeii threw the dripping towel at the bird, leaving a trail of yellow droplets across the room.

* * *

Later that afternoon, the doorbell rang while she still sponged remains of little puddles from the carpet. She struggled to her feet, towel in hand, and opened the door.

A young man stood on the covered porch. Slightly spiked, short black hair grew down into stylish sideburns. Dark eyelashes rimmed deep blue eyes set over a ski-slope nose and sensuous lips. He wore a pinstripe navy suit and maroon tie. The whole package resulted in an extremely good-looking man. And definitely not from Silverville.

"May I help you, young sir?"

"I'm looking for Pleasance Pantiwycke," he said. "Is she here?"

"Are you Italian?"

Looking perplexed, he answered, "Well, yes, but – "

Madame Pompeii threw the rag over her shoulder. "I knew it! Thank you, Guiding Spirits from the Great Beyond."

At that, she grabbed his lapels and yanked him through the door.

* * *

Madame Pompeii reentered the living room with a service tray carrying a pot of freshly brewed tea and two cups. Once again, her crystal ball had proven her powers as an adept. A nice young gentleman caller for her niece. And so handsome and polite. True, he'd seemed somewhat taken aback when she pushed him down in the chair. He wasn't going to wait, but she insisted that Pleasance would be back soon.

She placed the tray on the table, sat down opposite him, and poured. "Here's a nice cup of tea while we're waiting."

Glancing at his watch, he accepted the cup and smiled.

"Well now, where were we?" she asked. "Pleasance is my favorite niece, you know. Unfortunately, she shares none of my talent with arcane matters. Or much skill in the kitchen, but she can change the oil in her car in fifteen minutes, and she can bench-press 150 pounds."

He sat, quiet, and sipped the tea.

"Oh yes," she continued, "and Pleasance is well versed in art. She works for a museum in New York. She knows a lot about old things, always running around gathering material to put on display. Where did you say you were from? That doesn't mean the girl can't settle down. I've seen how she treats that dog over there." Madame Pompeii pointed to Proust, snoring in the corner. "So I know she'd be good with kids."

The young man looked at his watch again. "How much longer do you think it'll be?"

"I bet you're from Rome or Venice. But I have to say your English is very good."

"Actually I'm from –"

"But you have blue eyes. Well, I've heard that not everyone from Italy has brown. Was your mother from Norway? I've made a real study of runes and I've got a set in my bedroom. Would you like to see them?"

"Maybe I'll come back later." He started to rise.

Madame Pompeii jumped to her feet and pushed him back down. "Oh dear, I see the pot is almost empty. Let me go make us some fresh."

As she walked toward the kitchen, she turned over her shoulder. "My goodness, I never even asked your name."

"Cap," he said. "Cap Cappelli."

* * *

By the time the rain let up, Pleasance found herself near the end of the queue that lined up in a hall at the Galactic Inn, the film company's makeshift headquarters. Every now and again, people in line burst out in fits of singing – stanzas of "Copacabana" mingled with "The Way We Were" while lyrics from "Your Cheating Heart" drowned out strains of "Billie Jean." A loose chicken or two darted between owners' legs. But most people just waited patiently for their turn to interview.

Pleasance tapped the shoulder of the fat man in front of her.

"This is the line to apply for a film crew job, isn't it?"

"Sure is, little lady," he said, swiveling to face her. He thrust out a chubby hand. "Buford Price, town developer. And you are?"

He pumped her hand with a sweaty grip. A little too enthusiastic. She wiped her palm and replied, "Pleasance. I'm the niece of Perry –"

The man talked right over her words. "You wouldn't know by the looks of it now, but this town used to be completely dead – dead until I brought economic prosperity. Handed it to them on a silver platter. Why, I'm responsible for Alien Landing, the museum, and both the Fourth of July and Labor Day festivals."

He continued to recite his resume as Pleasance stepped out of line and let the two people at her back step forward. She slipped in behind the pair, a thin young man with a little boy.

"Thank you for letting us go ahead of you," the young man said.

"No problem."

She looked the pair over and thought she recognized them. It was hard not to forget the child, trussed up in a hooded sweatshirt and wearing sunglasses.

"Aren't you Howard Beacon?"

"Yes, ma'am."

"Applying for a job, too?"

"Yes, ma'am." Howard leaned over and pulled a flattened wad of gum off his shoe and showed it to the little boy, who nodded but said nothing. Howard fixed his gaze on the light fixture for several moments before he spoke again. "They're making a movie about what I saw."

Was he talking to her, to the child, or the light fixture? Oh, this was the guy that Aunt Lela pointed out when they drove back from Grady's. The kid had an odd name, but she didn't remember. "You saw aliens, right?"

"No, ma'am. All I saw was lights. But they left me a message."

"Really?"

"Yes. They told me that every place has windows and doors. You have to leave the doors open even if bugs fly in."

Still standing in front of Howard, Buford swung around and interrupted, "Here's what the aliens said: 'When Fate closes a door, it opens a window.'" He slapped Howard on the back. "You probably noticed that Silverville's celebrity isn't the sharpest tack in the carton."

Pleasance glanced to see if she could get any further back in the line, but decided it wouldn't be far enough.

Buford stooped to eyelevel with the boy. "So, who's your little friend, Howard? He applying for an alien part in the movie?" Buford laughed at what he must have thought was a clever comment.

"No, Mr. Price. Otto already has a job. He travels with –"

Just then, the film company door opened and a woman stepped out. "All the crew slots are now filled. Thanks to the rest of you for showing up today."

Disappointed "ohs" filled the hallway as people turned to leave.

The film company rep called after them, "Be sure to watch next summer for the premier of *Silverville vs. the Flying Saucers.* A big-screen invasion never to be forgotten!"

"What invasion?" Pleasance asked.

Buford leaned toward her. "For all we know, they're already among us. Ha-ha! And if they're not, who cares? We're making money off it. Say, what are you doing for dinner tonight?"

She veered away from the fat man's sour breath and escaped.

* * *

Pleasance took her eyes off the road long enough to read the card with the address for Telemarketing Enterprises. Giving her a card was the best the Chamber of Commerce could do when she'd inquired about local jobs after leaving the Galactic Inn. Not her typical line of work, but she needed operating capital, quick. And she dared not ask Winchester for another nickel.

She drove to the edge of town, past the city's new telescope. Like everything else in Silverville, the sign to the observatory featured aliens. Their big eyes peered through an enormous scope focused on Planet Earth. Another mile down the road, she approached a tin barn that looked like it'd been erected in a hurry. No sign, but this was the address. She parked beside a row of only three other cars, expecting to see more activity from prospective applicants. But the site was quiet. Pleasance circled the building until she found a door.

As she was about to enter, a woman burst out of the building, crying and bumping into her.

"What's wrong?" Pleasance asked.

The woman pushed passed, sobbing, "I feel like I need a shower."

Puzzled, Pleasance kept her hand on the open door while she watched the woman jump in her car and squeal out of the parking lot. What could possibly cause someone to have that kind of reaction? And why would anyone need a shower after working at a telemarketing firm? She shrugged it off and went inside.

A front desk sat before an array of eight cubicles lined up facing the far wall, phones ringing in each.

A toilet flushed and a familiar-looking man stepped through a small door at the side.

"You here for the job?" the man asked. "I just had someone quit. Can you start right now?"

"Now? Uh, what sort of —"

He thrust a sheet of paper into her hands. "Here's your script. Let me show you the set-up."

She followed him over to the cubicles. "Don't you want to know anything about my qualifications?"

"You're a woman and you can talk." He didn't even look back.

They passed the only other people in the building, a pair working inside one workstation. They both wore headsets.

The woman twirled her long blond hair, clearly bored, as she spoke into her microphone. "I'm not sure —"

"— we know how to do that," the man next to her added, brushing a crumb of pizza off his salt-and-pepper moustache. He spoke into the headset, "Maybe you should —"

"— explain just what you want," the blond said.

The supervisor led Pleasance to a desk and phone two cubicles further down the row. She motioned back at the couple. "Do they always do that — finish each other's sentences?"

"Annoying, isn't it?" The supervisor lowered his voice. "And they'll only work together. They say it's how they write, too."

"They're authors?"

"They think they are. Mark and Kym Todd. Guess they don't make enough money at it to quit their day jobs."

A chicken clucked from the chair before them, and the supervisor reached down with tender care and placed the bird on the floor. He pocketed two eggs sitting near the headset. "This is your workstation."

"What are we selling?"

"You just wait until the phone rings and follow your script. Of course, you're free to improvise in any way you want."

She seated herself at the desk and swung her chair around to face him. "I know where I've seen you. Didn't you work at the airport?"

"Still do. You almost need two jobs to make ends meet in Silverville."

"Oh, I remember. Your name is Pat."

"Mr. Montgomery to you, now that you work here." Without even asking her name, he returned to the front of the building.

The phone began to ring. She pulled on the headset, punched the first button with a flashing light, and picked up the script. She skimmed the first line: *Hi, this is Honeysuckle. I've been waiting for your call.*

"Hello? Hello?" the voice on the line asked.

"Uh, could you wait a minute?" She pressed the hold button and looked at the script again. Other phrases popped out at her. *I'm wearing a peekaboo negligee . . . Do you know what I'd like to do to you right now? . . . You're making me hot.*

She sat motionless for a moment, stood, and walked over to the other occupied cubicle. Mark was trimming his toenails while Kym systematically plucked gray hairs from her bangs as she stared at a compact mirror. Both continued to complete each other's sentences to their caller.

The conversation Pleasance overheard answered the question she was about to ask. No doubt about the kind of business offered by Telemarketing Enterprises. She headed toward the

82

door, pausing at the desk long enough to pitch Montgomery the script.

"You're selling phone sex."

"Duh. What did you think we were selling? Timeshares?"

"I can't do this." She started for the door.

"Wait!" Montgomery called out. "How 'bout a raise? I'll double the pay."

Pleasance kept walking. "I don't even know what I make now."

"I'll pay fifty dollars an hour."

She stopped. That was good money for Silverville. Since the film crew job was a bust, the most she could hope for was minimum wage, plus tips. "Okay, but you keep the chicken off my desk."

"Deal." He handed her back the script as she returned to her cubicle.

At best, this would be temporary work. Any day now, the rains would let up; she'd snatch the Spanish artifacts and book the first plane back to New York.

By the time she returned to her desk and replaced her headset, the first caller had hung up. But another light already flashed.

"Hi, this is Honeysuckle ..."

* * *

Her shift ended two hours after she started. Tomorrow would begin with full days. She'd need to plan ahead to use her lunch breaks to check on Grady. Her mind focused on these scheduling nuances as she parked the car and walked up the porch steps to the house.

Pleasance swung the door open. "I'm home! And I got that –"

She stopped in mid sentence. On the sofa sat a man with a face she thought she'd never see again.

In a song-song voice, her aunt announced, "You have a gentleman caller!"

Pleasance, without breaking stride, marched over as Cap stood. She gave him a long hug, followed by a hard slap across his face.

Madame Pompeii gasped and dropped her cup. "Pleasance! You dreadful child, where are your manners?"

Both Pleasance and Cap ignored her.

"I thought you were ..." *Dead.* Pleasance stopped short of saying the word, and ushered her aunt into her bedroom. "Aunt Penny, I need to talk to him alone."

"But, but...," Madame Pompeii sputtered as Pleasance closed the door on her shocked face.

When she returned to the living room, Cap stood in the exact place she'd left him.

"You're pissed."

"First, worried. Now, pissed," she shouted, invading his space and giving him little shoves backwards until he stumbled against the wall.

Cap glanced toward the hallway and lowered his voice. "Winchester was going to kill me. I had to drop out of sight."

"You couldn't spare time for a phone call?" she hissed.

"Not if I wanted to keep you out of this, and safe."

"And you decided to just turn up here?"

Proust, awakened by the outburst, waddled over to Pleasance and rooted her pant leg. One powerful thrust with her knee sent him scrambling out of the room.

"I'd heard you started working for Winchester. Not a good move, Pleasance."

"Oh, I get it. You came from God knows where to give me a warning." She couldn't keep the sarcasm out of her tone.

Cap slipped away from the wall and sat down while she pivoted, keeping him in eye-lock.

"I know you must have lots of questions, and I can answer some," he said. "Yes, I disappeared – I had to. The last heist Winchester sent me on set him back several hundred thousand dollars. There was no loot, no money left, no going back."

"You could have told me, Cap. I could've helped."

He shook his head. "No one can help when Winchester gets mad. This was the only way. I'm just sorry you're working for him now."

Holy shit. What had she gotten herself into? What would Winchester do to *her* if she didn't deliver on their contract?

Then she had another dark thought. "Why'd you really come here?"

"I could ask you the same thing. What're you doing in this piss-ant town?"

She knew why she was there, but that didn't explain Cap's sudden arrival – unless he'd gotten wind of the Spanish artifacts and was now trying to make himself part of the equation. Maybe he'd shown up more to redeem himself in Winchester's eyes than to give her a warning.

"I'm here visiting family."

"I don't buy it. No one walks away from Winchester, especially after a deal goes sour."

"How could you possibly know about Mexico? For that matter, how did you even know I was in Silverville?"

"I may be underground, but I hear things."

As far as Pleasance was concerned, that was the end of this part of the conversation. It had to be if she planned to keep her trade with Winchester.

She strained her face into a feminine, come-hither smile. She walked over and sat down on the couch next to him. "I'm glad you're not dead, Cap."

Cap twisted around to face her. "I did come here to warn you, Pleasance. But I also came here to see you. I've missed you."

The door to Madame Pompeii's bedroom squeaked open and her head soon popped around the living room entrance. "Time for more tea?"

"That'd be nice, Aunt Penny," Pleasance said. She leaned closer to Cap and whispered, "We can't talk here. Where are you staying?"

He shook his head. "Remember, I'm a dead man. Safer if you don't know."

"Then meet me tomorrow evening. Seven o'clock. A mile down the county road south of town."

* * *

Three days into her new job, Pleasance had improvised plenty. At first, she channeled the frustration of the job into anger at the customers – and to her surprise, they liked it. Everyone started to call for Honeysuckle. Honeysuckle, the Dominatrix.

"This is Honeysuckle, and this is what's going to happen to you," she'd bark. Next she would list all the demeaning tasks she required of her willing clientele.

"Get down and crawl, you slimy worm. Then lick the bottoms of your shoes."

"But I can't hold the phone while I'm crawling."

"Shut up, or I'll disconnect you!"

"Yes, Honeysuckle. Anything you say."

"That's *Ms*. Honeysuckle to you, turd face."

By the end of each shift, she found herself as invigorated as she'd been after a set of duels during her wrestling career.

On the morning of day four, Pleasance rummaged through the refrigerator before heading off to work. "I wish we had some eggs," she said to Uncle Perry as he entered the kitchen.

"Shhh! Not so loud. Lela might hear you."

"Oh, yeah. Sorry."

She grabbed a carton of milk and found a box of cereal in a nearby cupboard. She sat at the table and poured everything into a bowl. Perry joined her.

"You've sure seemed chipper the last couple of days," her uncle said. "That new job working out for you?"

Yeah, that and a few other things. Pleasance nodded and swallowed a mouthful of cereal. Now she just needed to figure out if the relationship with Cap went further than a mad tussle in the back seat of her car, trying to tear each other's clothes off. At first, she'd felt totally gob-smacked when Cap showed up at Perry and Lela's. She'd just come to terms with the possibility that he was either dead or else ditched her. A bit ashamed, she'd secretly hoped it was the first. But when she saw that grin smeared across his face, nonchalant and tracing a forefinger around the rim of his tea cup as though he'd just returned from an overnight trip – a torrent of unexpected emotions had scoured her senses. Relief that he was still alive, rage that he'd left her hanging. She'd needed to pummel him with her fists before she could grip him in a bear hug that he'd never escape.

Their rendezvous on the county road had led to an empty campground a few miles south of Silverville. After their passionate romp, Cap had tossed her a pre-paid disposable phone to call him on. It became clear they needed to find a different place to meet. The outskirts of town was too unpredictable, too unsecure. They'd decided to move their bedroom playground to a hotel in Placer City, a little town an hour away.

He still didn't know why she was in Silverville, and she wasn't sure she would tell him. She had to make good her own payback to Winchester, and she still had no idea what artifacts might be on Grady's ranch, or what they were worth. She couldn't risk sharing that information with Cap. Would he scoop her and try to get back into Winchester's good graces if he knew? But if Winchester already had offered a bounty on Cap's head, nothing could help him at this point.

No, she couldn't tell Cap the real reason she came to Silverville. As for his own reasons for coming, Pleasance would have to settle for what he'd said.

"Pleasance? Pleasance!" Uncle Perry waved a hand in front of her. "I asked you a question."

"Yes, what? I'm eating." Pleasance pushed her personal quandary to the back of her mind.

"I asked, What is it exactly you do at that phone job?"

Pleasance almost snorted at the thought. *I make men grovel in a kinky kind of way.*

"I'm sort of a self-help counselor."

Perry pulled the cereal and milk to his side of the table. "You mean like esteem issues?"

"You could say that. I give them suggestions and then it's up to them."

Perry smiled. "That's nice, Pleasance. You're a good girl."

She glanced at the clock on the wall. Still an hour before she had to leave. She stood anyway. "Sorry to cut this short, but I'm going to be late for work."

As she opened the front door, he shouted after her, "Don't make it too hard for them!"

But that's exactly what I'm paid to do, Uncle Perry. She laughed to herself. "See you tonight."

Once outside, Pleasance climbed into and started her new rental car, aiming it in the opposite direction of Telemarketing Enterprises. Twenty minutes later, she crouched on a bluff, training Perry's astronomy binoculars on Grady's ranch house a half-mile away. The rains had let up, and the clouds began to back off. Steam floated off soggy pastures warmed by the sun's rays, and pools of water sparkled across the ranch's rutted roads.

Surely that old fart would be heading out to the treasure site pretty soon. She glassed the buildings for any signs of activity, but all she saw was Leona hanging sheets on a clothesline. Pleasance maneuvered herself into a more comfortable position, careful not to muddy her clothes any more than she had already. Grady's pickup still sat in the yard, and the SUV hadn't moved from the bunkhouse.

The door of the main house opened, and Grady walked to his vehicle. Seconds later, the pickup fishtailed down the driveway for several hundred feet before veering off the gravel toward a rotting old shed. The truck slid sideways and careened past the building by a narrow miss. Then the passenger wheels dropped into a shallow ditch that ended Grady's progress with a halting lurch. The vehicle could do nothing but follow the depression, like a locomotive trapped by the confines of a track. Several times the old rancher rocked the truck back and forth to free it, but the wheels kept sliding back down. The door opened and Grady got out. Pleasance couldn't hear his words but she could guess from his body language what he was saying. He kicked the closest tire repeatedly and stomped back to the house.

Grady wouldn't be making a trip to the site today, and maybe not tomorrow either. Pleasance half slid, half skated down the slope of the bluff back to her car.

On the drive back to town, she realized she would need to keep a closer watch on the ranch as the ground began to dry. She'd also have to plan her maneuvers around her rendezvous with Cap. Once she found out the location of the treasure, she could determine what type of equipment she'd need, if any, to extract the Spanish artifacts. Uncle Perry probably still had decent rappelling ropes, a harness, and carabiners stashed with his climbing gear. On the other hand, the site might be easily accessible. She doubted that Grady would have offered to return the coins if the site had been difficult to reach. A shovel might be all she needed.

She reached the outskirts of town and turned onto Main Street. She'd traveled only a few blocks when the van in front of her pulled a sharp U-turn. Pleasance jammed on the brakes and steered clear, stopping just as the street light ahead turned red. The van, its paint job displaying a hot-air balloon, screeched to a stop at the opposite curb. Two men leaped out of the vehicle and threw a net over a couple of protesters making a scene at the fried-chicken restaurant. The men trussed up their captives and dragged them into the van, driving away at a brisk pace. The operation happened so fast that the stoplight hadn't had time to turn green.

And she thought New York was weird. At least she was used to that kind of crazy. She pressed the accelerator, almost sideswiping a black limousine parked on the side, and steered toward Telemarketing Enterprises.

* * *

Lela watched, stunned, from the back seat of a funeral limo with dark-tinted windows. She scooted forward and touched the driver's shoulder.

"Do you see what I mean? It's going to take desperate measures," she said.

In the days since she'd overheard City Council's plans to apprehend and contain the protesters, Lela had rallied a small and enthusiastic resistance group. They called themselves ATEP – the Association for the Triumph and Equality of Poultry. Of course, only those members who could hide their zeal had proven effective operatives in the field. They mingled with chicken-haters, masking their feelings while gathering intelligence. The group had also enlisted the help of a few sympathizers who hadn't yet experienced first-hand the affinity for fowl. Some became involved because they saw the City's policies as a gross encroachment on civil liberties. Like the two who now sat with her in the car. It didn't hurt that she'd also guilted them into helping. Two years ago, local undertaker Denton Fine and his wife, Felicia, had shared in another conspiracy to rid the town of tourists obsessed with aliens. Maybe *this* scheme would go more according to plan.

Except there was no concrete plan beyond initial surveillance.

"They've probably noticed us following them around," Denton said.

"I doubt it. They're too busy rounding up people." Lela pushed back and resettled into the plush rear seat. "This is the third group this morning."

She flipped open her cell phone and dialed the leader of the second reconnaissance team. "They just left Chicken Delight and are heading south on Main."

Felicia turned in the front seat. "Where do we go from here?"

Good question. The morning operation had helped the resistance group understand the procedures City Council used to capture victims and transfer them for detainment at the school gymnasium. Maybe the next step would be to case the holding facility for lapses in security. As far as she knew, no one had made provisions for the comfort of the detainees. But what really bothered her was the thought of helpless chickens held against their will, perhaps huddled in the corner of the gym on a hard, wooden floor. They needed to find a way to spring the prisoners.

"Head to the school."

* * *

Dream interpretation had never been Madame Pompeii's specialty. Even her own dreams. She sat up and threw back the covers, trying to piece together the fragmented images that visited her once again during the night. The latest dream had begun with Pleasance turning down one corner after another, each time blocked by one of the figures she'd seen in the crystal ball. But this time, there was a fifth man. Not the one she expected, Pleasance's new gentleman caller. This new dream figure wore a gold ring in his bottom lip.

The book she'd purchased the day before, *Dreams R Us*, lay on the nightstand. She picked it up and leafed through the pages, finding such categories as animals, themes, characters, and relationships. Settling on characters, she found a section called "Men." The entry explained that male images could indicate masculine aspects of the self – assertiveness, aggression, competiveness. That certainly described Pleasance, but Madame Pompeii saw nothing prophetic in the descriptions. Because the dreams seemed threatening, she tried the entry on "Enemies." But opposing ideas and inner conflicts didn't really fit either. She tossed the book on the bed.

None of the categories described what she dreamt, and certainly none matched what she saw in the crystal ball.

The three Latin men were easy enough to explain, but she still shivered at the thought of the fourth figure – a disturbing demonic force, she felt sure. And now came the fifth individual. What had Pleasance gotten herself into? And how did Mr. Cappelli fit into the picture?

Her own pivotal role in solving the conundrum of the curse had given her confidence in her awakening psychic abilities. So why couldn't she decipher these dreams about Pleasance? She did feel that everything she'd been seeing in her visions had a suggestion of hidden malevolence. Perhaps the recent fury with which Ptolemy scratched Lela's furniture was really a veiled message, a metaphor for tackling the problem head on. Of course, Madame Pompeii couldn't tackle what she didn't understand.

Slipping on her new green and yellow muumuu, she pasted a fresh star to her forehead and prepared a cup of turnip tea. Five men in the dreams. Every time Pleasance turned a corner, one of them blocked her way. On the other hand, she once had a dream about five oranges, and nothing ever came of that. Maybe the significance wasn't the men but the number five. Five people lived in the household – well, four actually, but the cat and the dog and the bird probably equaled one person. Pleasance had to be in her mid-twenties by now, and she might be as young as twenty-three. Two plus three equaled five again. Pleasance had five fingers on each hand and five toes on each foot. The previous night she'd watched Pleasance eat five slices of pizza in a row. And the girl also answered "five" when Perry asked what time she got off work that night.

Yes, five must be the significant element of her visions. Five points adorned the edges of a pentagram, and a pentagram was a source of protection. That must be the key! Either Pleasance had protection, or else she needed it.

Time to consult with a fellow psychic. Time to visit Kandy-B-Good.

CHAPTER EIGHT

When Madame Pompeii arrived at the tent, the sign, "Kandy-B-Good – Possessions, Auras, and Other Weird Stuff," no longer adorned the wall. The girl's fame had probably grown to the point that she no longer needed to advertise. She peered inside, where a young woman crouched near packed boxes, stuffing strings of beads into the only carton still open. Gone were the balloons, pillows, and Teddy bear.

"Excuse me," Madame Pompeii interrupted. "I'm looking for Kandy."

The young woman stood and faced her. "I'm Candace."

It couldn't be. This person no way resembled the extraordinary psychic she'd met only two weeks before. Her wardrobe consisted of a smart tweed skirt and matching jacket. High-heeled shoes complemented the Gucci handbag slung over her shoulder. Stylish short hair completed the corporate image. Still, the face looked the same.

"Candace? As in Kandy B. Good?"

With a cynical laugh, the new Kandy once again stooped to continue packing. "In a previous life, maybe."

Madame Pompeii stood just inside the tent, gawking at the new incarnation of her former confidante. She hardly knew what to say. This unexpected persona placed a barrier between their psyches.

The remade Kandy closed the container and straightened up. "Do you want some of this stuff?"

"I – I need your advice on something."

"Sorry. Closed for business. You'll have to get your hoo-doo somewhere else."

Madame Pompeii gasped. The young seer must have turned away from the Calling, denying her gift of spiritual sight. Perhaps she'd crumbled under the weight of knowing people's fates. Or perhaps she, too, had encountered the unsettling figure in the crystal ball. Whatever it was, something horrible must have happened to her.

"Kandy, surely you're not walking away from the Inner Circle?"

From the height of her three-inch heels, Kandy looked down at her. "You mean the Circle of Crap? Don't tell me you believe in all that? And it's Candace now."

"Of course, I still believe. It's The Path of Truth."

Candace pulled a compact mirror out of her bag and smoothed her hair. "The only path I'm interested in is the one to Hollywood. I'm now assistant to the producer of *Silverville vs. the Flying Saucers*."

"You can't be serious! What could possibly make you forsake The Path for something as superficial as a movie?"

"About fifty grand. Now if you'll get out of *my* path, I'm going to be late for work."

Candace pushed past Madame Pompeii, handing her the box of beads as the young woman stepped through the tent door.

* * *

"Thank you, my good man," Maurice said. He fingered the coins Mr. O'Grady had just given him, extricating a loupe from his vest pocket. "And these came from the same site as the other artifacts?"

"Yep."

As the two stood on the front doorstep of the ranch house, Maurice studied the coins with the magnified end of the loupe. Ah, yes, the Maltese cross stamped on one side and the shield of the House of Hapsburg on the other. He'd seen these before. Although the state of preservation lacked much to be desired. Nonetheless, the thought of retrieving the remaining *objets d'arts* before Pleasance or anyone else had a chance to lay claim to them gave him inestimable pleasure. And the time for retrieval must come soon.

In the meantime, to Maurice's delight the appearance of Pleasance's paramour had raised the stakes in the game. Pleasance had never noticed Maurice watching from the hill above her during her own surveillance sorties. But while she secretly observed Mr. O'Grady, her young man spied on her, and Maurice covertly watched them all. Obviously, she planned to scoop Mr. Cappelli by keeping track of the rancher's quotidian movements. Poor naïve young people. This was so much more complicated than she or her returned lover realized.

"Might we be in a position to reclaim the other objects in the next day or two?" Maurice asked Grady as he returned the loupe to his pocket.

"Maybe."

"Perhaps you could be more precise?"

The rancher spit a wad of tobacco at the cur circling their legs. "Ain't gonna happen today. Them rains most likely caused a mudslide over the mouth of the cave we need to get to."

"Most unfortunate. Is there perchance a solution for this impasse to our progress?"

The disgusting mongrel shoved its filthy snout against Maurice's pant leg, and he slipped a hand into his pocket, the same pocket that hid the taser. The dog must have remembered and leaped off the porch.

"What the hell!" Mr. O'Grady pushed his hat back on his forehead.

Maurice ignored the dog's reaction, shuffling toward the door. "Shall we step inside to discuss the details of the excavation?" To the octogenarian's surprise, the rancher stepped to block his way.

"No, sir. Not with them coins in your hands."

"I was hoping for another cup of your wife's extraordinary Lipton's tea."

Mr. O'Grady didn't move.

Maurice shrugged. "Yes, well, we can make our arrangements in *plein air*, if you prefer. Will we require any special equipment?"

"Just shovels and a couple of strong backs."

How vulgar. Maurice seldom resorted to physical exertion. He usually left that distasteful task to underlings. "Are you suggesting that such an endeavor may require additional assistance?"

The rancher's eyes scanned Maurice from head to toe and paused on the walker. "I reckon so since you ain't gonna be much help."

"Excellent idea, Mr. O'Grady. I, of course, will provide the remuneration for whomever you employ. We can be assured of their discretion, I presume?"

"Won't be a problem if we find somebody who don't know much English."

* * *

Pleasance adjusted the headset and punched the next blinking button. "This is Honeysuckle, and this is what's going to happen to you."

The caller on the line paused and said in broken English, "Um, ja, ist dis Fräulein Honeysuckle?"

"Yes, you German sausage-whacker!"

"*Gut, gut*. You like the German sausage then?"

"Only boiled, flayed, or skewered. Now take off those Lederhosen straps and wrap them around your ankles."

"*Ach*! I betcha you are a real *heisse Nummer*, a hottie!"

"You bet your curry würst, Adolf. And don't expect any mercy!"

"*Scheisse! Meine Frau kommt.* I gotta go! *Auf Wiedersehn.*"

She'd gotten used to that kind of interrupted sign-off when the wife came home, and in lots of different languages.

She connected to the next caller. "This is Honeysuckle, and this is what's going to happen to you."

"*Oui! Oui!*"

"Wee-wee is the least you'll do when I'm done with you."

She launched into the usual repertory that Frenchmen seemed to prefer, this time adding a bit of her signature flourish with berets and baguettes.

And so the morning went.

A few hours later, she looked at her watch. Almost noon. The button began blinking again, and she decided to take one more call before she broke for lunch.

"This is Honeysuckle, and this is what's going to –" On the other end of the line she heard several men bickering, then a slap, and someone yelped.

Oh great, cheapskates. Trying to get their jollies for the price of one. She waited until the din died down and someone spoke.

"*¿Hola?*"

"How many of you do I have to punish today?"

"*Son tres.* You must punish three of us."

"Give me a name so I know which one to humiliate first." Of course, no one ever gave their real names.

"My name eez Lorenzo."

Again, she heard a slap and yelp. In the background, one of the others barked, "Don't give her your real name, *estúpido!*"

"I mean, my name is Mocoso."

Another slap, and a louder yelp as she heard the same background voice growl, "*¡Dios mío!* Not my name either!"

Lorenzo, Mocoso – couldn't be. She could see them all in her mind's eye, standing in the jungle shanty. Mocoso, the short, ugly one. And very dangerous. Lorenzo with the wild, curly hair. And what was that third one's name? The fat, bald one. Oh yes. She asked, "Is there someone named Rizoso with you?"

She heard the phone juggle as Lorenzo said, "It's for you, Rizoso."

"*Soy* Rizoso. You have heard of me?"

Pleasance froze. Tomás did tell them she was in Silverville after they'd tortured him. They must be setting a trap for her. No, they were too stupid. Or were they? Maybe their stupidity was a ploy, meant to catch her off guard while they bartered for the Mayan artifacts. Still, they'd gone to jail for robbing a bank at a drive-up window. That wouldn't have exactly put them at the head of the smart queue. And they couldn't have guessed she was the one taking this call. It was a 900 number. No, they couldn't know she was their phone-sex operator.

She relaxed and let Honeysuckle take over. "Everyone's heard of Rizoso, Mocoso, and Lorenzo." She added, "Of course, everyone also knows that Rizoso is the best lover."

Pleasance didn't have to see her caller to know that his chest swelled as he turned to tell the other two what she'd just said. She heard more fighting, and another voice came on the line.

"No, *señorita*, Mocoso is the best lover."

"Let's see which one of you best obeys orders." Time to have a little more fun than usual. Then she thought of Tomás and his maimed hand. Because of Mocoso, Lorenzo, and Rizoso, he would never go bowling again. "Who's standing next to you?"

"Rizoso."

"Grab his little finger and bend it back as far as you can."

Within seconds the phone must have hit the floor, and someone shouted in pain.

"Okay, *señorita*, what next?" Mocoso asked.

"Knock Lorenzo to the ground and bite off his earlobe."

Another scuffle crackled through the headset, and this time it took longer for Mocoso to return to the phone. She heard spitting sounds as he said, "It is done. You see, I am the best one taking orders. Lorenzo! Put down that wrench! *Señorita*, can you hold, *por favor*?"

The phone went dead.

If they called back again, she might not be as easy on them. Good lord, what were the chances those three would call a 900 number and get her? Aunt Lela had once mentioned that strange coincidences seemed to occur in Silverville. But if these jokers routinely indulged in telephone erotica, it made sense that they might eventually call Telemarketing Enterprises. Of course they would, and Pleasance chocked the whole incidence up to unlikely but not strange. Well, not strange in this town.

From the other cubicle, the Todds shouted in unison, "Line two for Honeysuckle!"

Pleasance punched the button.

Before she could speak, the client on the other end said, "I'd love to kiss that little mole on your left breast." Then heavy breathing.

She laughed at Cap's teasing voice on the line. "Why didn't you call the cell?"

"Why didn't *you* call the cell?"

Maybe because I've been sitting on a rock in my spare time, trying to catch an old geezer before he sticks his hands in the antiquities cookie jar.

"Still on for tonight?" he asked.

"Yep, I'll be there. Placer City Super 8, six-thirty."

"Bring some kinky toys from work."

"Kinkiest thing here is Pat's chicken, and I doubt he'd loan it out for the night."

"Then I'll just have to settle for you. See you in a few hours." The line disconnected.

She removed her headset, leaned back, and stretched. All things considered, it had been a good morning, and promised to be a better evening. She looked forward to a larger-than-average lunch. Maybe Mexican food.

* * *

"If I smoked, I'd need a cigarette." Pleasance stretched, sighed, and kicked at the sheet that had tangled around her ankles during the intensity of the last hour.

Cap didn't move, eyes closed and smiling.

"How 'bout a glass of Pinot Noir instead?" Rolling off the bed, he reached for a duffel bag and produced a tall, slender bottle and a cork screw.

"From the bottle?" she asked.

"Course not. Only the finest for you. " He stood and walked toward the bathroom, his naked butt muscular and firm with each stride. Wide shoulders supported a strong neck that tapered into thick, black hair. A perfect match to his nude beach tan. God, he was beautiful.

She glanced down at her own stockier frame, almost as masculine as his. Other men had found her beautiful although she never considered herself so. She'd often puzzled over why Cap had become attracted to her. His was a physique that could capture the attention of any woman – and no doubt it had, countless times. How many had he been with during his disappearance? She wouldn't think about that.

He came back with two plastic cups and handed her one. He extracted the cork from the bottle and poured. "To us."

She took one of the cups. "To us."

Is there an "us"? She didn't know how there could be. The timing sucked. Cap was on the run and couldn't commit to a relationship. Nor could she, not with her immediate future clamped in a vise twisted by Winchester. Pleasance needed to focus on putting together a black market package that had nothing to do with her fugitive lover. Her life depended on it – or at least that's what Winchester implied. A slight tremor in her hand sent ripples across the surface of the dark red liquid in her cup.

Cap set his wine on the table. "Too bad we couldn't risk meeting at the Galactic Inn." He gestured at the franchise furnishings surrounding the bed – stereotypical southwest art prints, a pot meant to look Navajo but probably made in China. "I hear the ambiance is far more entertaining."

Pleasance had heard that, too, from Perry and Lela. How pseudo Jetsons' décor filled the rooms and saucer-like lamps hung near beds, suspended on thin cords. Eerie pictures of alien landscapes accented the walls, and floating ringed planets adorned the bed covers.

"In all my travels," he continued, "I've never seen such a screwball place as Silverville. You know the story behind all that alien stuff?"

She shrugged. "Only that a local might have seen a UFO a few years ago. Someone got the bright idea of keeping the legend alive."

"And the chickens?"

She set her cup on the dresser, rolled over, and groaned. "Don't even ask."

"Why is Silverville even there? I didn't see a railroad or anything."

"Guess there used to be. All torn out now."

"Bet there's a lot of history there."

Pleasance sat up and struggled into a t-shirt. "Must have been. Aunt Lela said the Old Spanish Trail came right through –" She swallowed the rest of the sentence, fearing where the conversation could lead. Sharing more might place her in danger, him in danger, or both of them. "Why so suddenly interested?"

That disarming grin spread over Cap's face. "Just wondering about all the frontier history, adventurers heading West and seeking their fortune. No reason."

She hoped he wasn't fishing. Before she said something she'd regret, she needed to derail talking about Silverville so he didn't figure out why she was really there.

"I have a better way to spend the evening than talking about history." Pleasance peeled her t-shirt back off. "Less talk, more sex."

* * *

Pleasance felt ravenous the next morning. She'd wanted more than Super 8's continental breakfast, and at first light she dragged Cap down to the local greasy spoon for biscuits and gravy. While she plunged her fork into the runny eggs on top, Cap toyed with a short stack of pancakes.

"Not hungry?"

"Not much of a breakfast-eater."

He seemed distracted.

"You're leaving again, aren't you?" she asked.

He nodded. "You know I can't stay in one place too long. I need to drop out of sight again."

Maybe just as well. This way she'd never have to tell him about the Spanish artifacts, and she'd never have to know if he intended to deceive her.

Cap set the fork down. "In the meantime, you've got to find a way to get out of Winchester's clutches. How are you going to placate him after Mexico?"

"Silverville is just a sabbatical. I have a plan."

"What plan?"

"Don't worry about me. I can take care of myself."

The waitress arrived to refill their coffee cups. When she left, Cap said, "Make sure that you do. Don't end up like me."

He doesn't suspect. "Maybe I can find a crashed spaceship. An alien maybe."

"I'm serious."

"I know." She reached across the table and stroked his hand. "But you've got your own problems. Like staying alive."

Cap frowned and shook his head. He seemed unconvinced. Or maybe he was still holding something back.

Just like she was.

* * *

Only eighteen inches separated Pleasance's braids from Maurice's fedora – mauve, of course. A bit of accent to his disguise. Fortunately, Pleasance's back had been to the door when he'd entered the dismal little eatery and occupied the adjacent booth. Since Mr. Cappelli had no idea who he was, Maurice had the good fortune to situate himself propitiously close without notice.

He'd watched for days the regularity of her routine. But when she'd suddenly left town the previous day, Maurice felt compelled to follow. Pleasance hadn't detected his presence when he tailed her. Nor had she discovered that he'd taken the adjoining room at the hotel in Placer City. With the stethoscope he employed against the wall, Maurice gathered useful tidbits between their groans and a continuously squeaking bed.

Now he sat quietly in the plastic-covered seat to overhear the conversation in the adjacent booth. From the lovers' cryptic conversation at breakfast, he'd garnered additional gleanings, and he'd learned enough to know that Pleasance had positioned herself in a most precarious circumstance. It might, at some point, even require his intervention so that she could continue to play the game.

For the second time, the establishment's waitress arrived at his booth. He'd managed to wave her off the first time without speaking, but now she had the audacity to persist.

She tapped the menu before him. "If you sit here, you gotta order."

Maurice couldn't risk Pleasance hearing his voice. With haste he pointed to a garish picture of indefinable fare.

"Okay, pigs in a blanket it is." She walked brusquely toward the kitchen.

Pigs in a blanket? A most peculiar locution for something purported to be edible. As soon as the waitress disappeared through the door, Maurice scooted out from the booth and made his escape.

* * *

Lela flipped open her ringing cell phone.

"They're on their way to Ed's Wing Bucket," the second reconnaissance team leader reported. "They should be here by 1600."

"Copy that." Lela snapped the phone shut, and turned to Denton, who drove Recon One. "Ed's Wing Bucket. Come on, we gotta move now!"

The operation was going according to plan.

Originally, Lela had hoped to spring the prisoners from the gym, but after casing the joint, they found too much security, two guards placed at each door. The group settled on Plan B. Risky and illegal, it made them all a little uncomfortable, but they felt they had no choice.

"Duke and Felicia, is the gear ready?" Lela asked.

The two nodded from the back of Duke's AMC Gremlin, bouncing off each other every time the hatchback squealed around a corner. Denton and Felicia had talked their son into joining the resistance group since he was killing time the summer before he started pre-med school. And his car provided another vehicle for surveillance.

Plan B had involved baiting Bob Hardin with a false tip about demonstrators marching in front of the Wing Bucket. Once he and Arno Aasfresser, his assistant, showed up, the operation would be over in minutes.

Lela felt a little sorry about what would soon happen to Bob. Arno, on the other hand, deserved everything he'd get. The slimy little foul-mouthed creep. Always difficult to work with, particularly when she'd served as mayor, Arno acted like he ran the city instead of just the dog pound. Not long ago, when she'd taken Proust for a walk in the city park, Lela had turned the dog loose to run around the softball bleachers. Within thirty seconds, Arno showed up in his dogcatcher wagon and chewed her out for not obeying the city leash laws. He dropped a net over Proust – the same one they now used to capture chicken demonstrators – and despite her protests, hauled the dog to the city shelter. It cost Lela a hundred and twenty dollars to bail the pug out of doggie jail. All the while Arno smirked as he collected the money. Now it would be Lela's turn to smirk.

Recon One arrived at the scene just as members of the second team stood at the curb. They were pointing out the public restroom at the side of the building to Bob and Arno, who strode toward the closed door.

Lela and company tumbled out of the hatchback and ran over to their co-conspirators.

"Where are they going?" Lela asked, a little breathless.

"We told Bob the protesters had to go to the bathroom."

"You told him what?"

"We figured it would be easier to corner them in there."

"Concealment visors!" Lela shouted. Both recon teams pulled paper sacks over their heads and dashed toward the door.

A member of the second team stumbled as he swiveled the sack around his head, shouting, "I forgot to poke eyeholes!" He bounced off Denton and started to run at the wall of the brick building. Felicia veered to intercept the errant stray.

"Leave him!" Lela barked. "Stay on task."

The resistance team ignored their blinded comrade and made a beeline toward the bathroom. The commotion alerted Bob and Arno, who turned and faced the seven sack-headed storm troopers. Before either of them could react, Lela's group pushed them both through the door and rushed inside behind them.

"What's going on?" Bob demanded as he pitched toward the urinal.

Lela's kidnappers worked with speed and efficiency in the single-serve bathroom despite the limited space. They snatched away the nets, trussed up the captives, and pushed them to the floor.

Arno started to whine, "Please, please, I have a wife and kids."

"You people are insane." Bob struggled against the net. "What do you think you're doing?"

"We have to gag the prisoners," Lela said in a low voice, trying to disguise her identity, "especially this one." She dug the toe of her shoe into Arno's ribs.

Denton reached for the paper towel dispenser and pulled out a single sheet. "There's only one."

"Stuff it in Bob's mouth." Lela plucked a bar of soap off the sink. "This is for Arno."

Arno's eyes grew bigger as the bar approached his mouth. "No! Please! Not that filthy thing!"

Lela pinched Arno's nose until he took a breath and stuffed the scummy gag into his mouth. She held her hand against his lips so he couldn't spit it out and turned to the group.

"The blindfolds," Lela said, "who's got the blindfolds? We're going to need them to keep the gags in."

All the paper sacks looked at each other. Then one said, "We forgot them."

"What are we going to use?" Lela asked.

Duke's paper sack scanned the interior of the bathroom. He checked in the cupboard under the sink, rummaged through the trashcan, and finally squeezed past the nine bodies – two on the floor -- and into the only stall.

He returned with a roll of toilet paper. "This'll work."

Duke straddled Bob. "I'm afraid I'm going to have to ask you to hold still."

"Wrap their whole heads so they can't see," Lela said, tossing Duke a package of masking tape. "Hold them, men."

Duke commenced to wrap half a roll of toilet tissue around Bob's head, securing it with several strips of tape at the base of the neck.

Lela smirked with satisfaction after Duke repeated the same for Arno.

* * *

Maurice sat shotgun in Mr. O'Grady's truck, holding a handkerchief to his face. The acrid aroma of recent horse manure wafted from the insteps of the rancher's boots each time he stomped on the brake or pedaled the clutch to change gears. Maurice wished he'd had the forethought to splash *eau de cologne* on his handkerchief.

The old pickup bounced over drying ruts that laced the dirt road, one time jolting open Maurice's door from a particularly precarious bump.

"Been meaning to fix that," Mr. O'Grady said, not even slowing down.

Keeping his left hand clamped to his nose, Maurice reached over with the right one to refasten the door.

The pickup turned onto the highway, rattling up to speed. Dislodged clods of mud clattered against the wheel wells, soon replaced by the jangling of misaligned tires.

Maurice raised his voice to be heard. "Are you fairly certain that we can secure the assistance of workers for the next few days?"

Mr. O'Grady shrugged, or maybe just struggled to keep the steering wheel straight.

Maurice persisted, "Does this employment service you spoke of recommend discrete individuals of the highest caliber?"

The rancher laughed, spitting a stream of tobacco juice, most of which exited the truck window. "All kinds, I reckon. We'll get the hard-luck cases, most likely."

Maurice nodded, although Mr. O'Grady never looked in his direction.

The rancher shouted over the road noise, "One thing's for sure, we ain't hiring no locals. Don't want no one blabbering about where the cave is."

"Won't that rather limit our options?"

"Yep."

Disconcerting, to say the least. Maurice hoped to complete his sojourn in Silverville with a minimum of delay once the excavation could begin.

The pickup passed the city limits and continued through town toward Main Street. Mr. O'Grady turned onto a side road and parked a half block from the principle thoroughfare.

"Here we are," Mr. O'Grady said.

Maurice scanned a row of nondescript buildings. "Where?"

The rancher pointed at an inauspicious door with small red lettering stenciled onto the glass: "Silverville County Job Service." To the left, an equally plain plate-glass window adorned the stucco-finished exterior wall, revealing glimpses of an interior waiting room filled only with empty chairs.

"But where are all the potential employees?" Maurice asked.

Grady crawled out of the truck. "At home waiting for a phone call, I s'pose."

The door on Maurice's side of the vehicle caught on its hinges halfway open. The octogenarian squeezed through the exit and hobbled to the truck bed to retrieve his walker when he saw that Mr. O'Grady had made no move to get it for him.

By the time Maurice arrived at the Job Service entrance, the rancher had stepped inside with the door already slamming shut.

"Excuse me, sir," Maurice heard a voice say.

A preposterous looking woman approached him on the sidewalk. She wore a gaudy muumuu painted with stars and crescent moons.

"Have we met before?" she asked.

Maurice would certainly remember an encounter with such a remarkable specimen. The woman's black and white streaked hair hung in ropes beneath a flowered hat, and the points of the star on her forehead had begun to curl with sweat.

He bowed slightly. "Why no, Madame. I don't believe we have."

"I'm sure I've seen you, and recently. Are you another adept? With a booth at the theme park?"

He stifled a laugh. "I'm not unfamiliar with the arcane arts, but alas, I am not."

The boorish woman continued to study his face. "Then maybe at the new hairdresser's in town?"

"I assure you that we haven't –"

"I sense some deeper connection between us." She took a step closer and reached for his hand. "Maybe I should read your palm."

But the moment she touched him, a little cry escaped her lips and she staggered backwards. "You shocked me!"

Maurice dropped his hand back into his jacket pocket. "You must excuse me. I have pressing business inside this establishment. Good day."

He left her wide-eyed standing on the sidewalk and hurried inside.

Mr. O'Grady stood before a counter. On the other side a tall, thin woman studied a sheet of paper, her glasses halfway down her nose. She looked up at the rancher. "Well, I'm not sure I understand exactly what you need. You don't want local people?"

Mr. O'Grady shifted from foot to foot. "Well, you know. Maybe someone without papers."

A slow look of realization crept over the woman's face. "Oh, you want *illegals*. You don't want to pay a decent wage."

"Ma'am, I aim to pay –"

"I'm sorry, Mr. O'Grady." She dropped the sheet into a folder on the counter and slammed it shut. "We can't help you."

The job service representative stormed through a door at the rear of the room, leaving both men alone.

Mr. O'Grady turned to Maurice. "Looks like we're on our own."

"You mean to excavate?"

"Naw, I mean to find some help." Mr. O'Grady pushed his hat back to reveal an upper forehead white and untouched by the sun. "I got a neighbor who hired some boys from out of town, but he won't likely spare them with haying season almost here."

Maurice watched the leathery old cowboy attempt to formulate an alternative plan, behavior evidently foreign to him, as his normally vacuous expression transformed into a visage of intense absorption. The octogenarian prompted, "An inquiry or two by phone might be in order at this point."

"Yep, let's head back to the ranch."

* * *

The ride to the ranch seemed quiet despite the groaning complaints of the antiquated pickup's engine. Mr. O'Grady never spoke at all, but he scratched his ear and his lip twitched. No doubt the result of an overtaxed cerebral cortex.

"Have any inspirations come to mind?" Maurice asked.

"Kinda hard to think with you bothering me."

Maurice had only encountered such labored concentration in one other person, in the dilapidated home of a rather obtuse individual from Custer, South Dakota. The oaf had recently quit his job after winning five-thousand dollars from a lottery ticket. But he soon discovered that monetary pittance insufficient to live on. Yet he still had the impudence to insist on full market value for a rare Star Wars Pez dispenser. Just like Mr. O'Grady, the man's face displayed the same demonstrative effort of unaccustomed deliberation.

The truck chugged along the highway. Maurice hoped the rancher could think and drive at the same time.

Without warning, the vehicle veered to miss hitting three men standing beside an old car pulled to the side of the road. Mr. O'Grady slowed.

"Them's our boys."

"Pardon me?"

"The fellers waving on the road."

The pickup came to rest right in front of a vintage Chrysler Imperial, rusted from fender to fender. Smoke billowed from a raised hood. The three men beside the vehicle smiled, apparently relieved that assistance was at hand.

Maurice squinted through the mud-encrusted windshield at the curious trio. There was something familiar about them. In the Yucatán, in the dark leafy jungles, just outside a tin-sided shanty.

Mr. O'Grady rolled down his window and called back to them. "Looks like you boys need some help."

A man with a black bowl haircut trotted over to the driver side of the pickup. "*Sí, señor. Muchas gracias.* Our car, she is broken."

When the other two followed, the black-haired man turned and pushed one of them into the other, causing both men to stumble and fall. "*Ándele!* I do the talking!"

Ah, yes, the leader of the three inept thieves. Maurice had caught but a glimpse of the men, but their buffoonish behavior was unmistakable. They, of course, never detected his presence that day in Xlohil as he covertly replaced their jade mask with a grape-flavored Pez. The jade mask they thought Pleasance had stolen. No doubt these stranded wayfarers had also discovered Pleasance's whereabouts. The sheer coincidence of this chance meeting on the road was nothing short of fortuitous luck.

"Need a tow?" Mr. O'Grady offered.

Maurice leaned across the cab and whispered, "Aren't we going to engage their services?"

The rancher jerked his head back toward Maurice just long enough to say, "I'm gettin' to that. Let me do the talking." Mr. O'Grady pushed open his door and stepped outside.

Maurice settled back in his seat to allow the two "talkers" to negotiate. Fortuitous indeed. The presence of the thieves could provide maneuverable distraction, perhaps even frighten Pleasance away long enough for him to conclude his business. Maurice smiled at the possibilities. The situation called for a modicum of subtlety. If his feminine counterpart – if one could call Pleasance feminine – didn't take flight once she saw the thieves, he might arrange for an interesting little *tête-à-tête* for the four of them. He would, of course, make every attempt to avoid orchestrating an encounter involving violence – against the hopelessly ill-prepared men. Pleasance required no protection. At least from these fellows.

Mr. O'Grady rattled a tow chain from a toolbox. Maurice twisted to watch the rancher hook the chain to the undercarriage of the Chrylser while the dark-haired man climbed behind the wheel.

The other two jumped into the bed of the pickup, displaying large toothy smiles at Maurice through the window. One wore a bandage over his ear, the other a splint on his finger.

He straightened forward in the seat, plucked a sanitary wipe from his pocket, and dabbed his face and hands. From the back glass he heard a knock, which he chose to ignore.

Mr. O'Grady returned to the cab and started the engine.

"I take it you made the necessary arrangements for their employ?" Maurice asked.

"Yep."

"And the car? We're transporting it to a mechanic in town?"

"Nope. Gonna fix it myself. You're paying for the parts."

"And what of the men in the meantime?"

Grady ground the pickup into gear. "They're bunking with you."

CHAPTER NINE

The seven sack-headed chicken sympathizers stood around the coop watching their hostages eat tamale TV dinners for breakfast. Lela's turn to feed Bob and Arno. She'd hoped to serve up the last of the grits, but Pleasance had gotten hold of the box ahead of Lela, which meant there were no leftovers. All she could find at the spur of the moment was frozen Mexican food.

The captives sat on mattresses Duke had dragged into the coop for makeshift beds. Chickens skirted along the outside edges of the enclosure, clucking indignantly at this intrusion into their usual living space. Luckily for Bob and Arno, the coop sat in one corner of a sturdy barn. And luckily for the recon team, the barn sat on the outskirts of town far from the ears of rescuers.

"You could have at least microwaved these first," Arno complained, crunching on a brittle tortilla.

Yes, Lela wished she'd remembered to do that. But the role of poultry police was distracting and unfamiliar, and she couldn't think of everything.

Felicia touched Lela on the shoulder and whispered, "Has anyone gotten back to you yet about the exchange?"

Lela shook her besacked head no. The previous night, she'd called the dispatch switchboard and conveyed their demands for an exchange of hostages.

"I vant you to tell the mayor," Lela said, trying make her voice sound Russian, "ve have heese dog-catcher henchmen. If he vants to see them again, he must trade for the preesinors in the geem."

"Hold on," the dispatcher said. "I'll connect you with Mayor Jackson."

"Nyet! Nyet!"

Lela hung up, afraid that Earl Bob would recognize her voice. But now she wasn't sure that he'd gotten the message. She didn't even have a chance to lay out the instructions for the exchange.

Lela pulled Felica away from the group and told her what had happened on the phone. "We need to get everyone together to talk about our next step."

They walked back toward the others, who watched Arno shovel rice into his mouth.

"Helen – I mean, 003 – can we use your kitchen?" Lela asked, motioning the others to follow her outside.

They single-filed into the old farmhouse and seated themselves around the table.

Duke pulled the sack from his head. "I think we should consider waterboarding to make them talk."

"Don't be ridiculous," Felicia scolded. "Besides, what could they tell us that we don't already know?"

Lela added, "This isn't that type of operation. We just need to figure out a way to let our demands be known."

She repeated the phone fiasco to the group. "Earl Bob is going to recognize any of our voices if dispatch transfers us to him. We've got to think of another way."

Denton drummed his fingers on the table. "Well, we could spell out the message from newspaper letters and drop it off at the police station."

"As they take you into custody?" Felicia asked.

"Mail it just to Earl Bob then?"

"No good," Lela said. "That would take too long."

Then 003 raised her hand. "I know. We could catch one of the pigeons at City Park and tape the message to its leg."

"These aren't homing pigeons, Helen," Lela said. "The bird would probably just fly off."

The room grew silent with thought. Finally, Lela stood and smiled.

"There's one other possibility."

"What? What?" the others chimed together.

"All we need is our paper sacks, a couple of Madame Pompeii's muumuus, some tin foil, and a tape recorder."

* * *

Maurice poured a fine Beaujolais Cru over the chicken, mushrooms, and pearl onions simmering in the skillet, trying to focus his full attention on the permeating bouquet. Anything to distract him from the ruffians who lounged on the couch behind him. Such a pity that the accommodations would not allow privacy for his evening repast.

He and his three new bunkmates would share a single large room until they retrieved the treasure. A hotel was out of the question, although he'd considered it. Now was not the time to allow any aspect of the pending excavation to proceed without his direct supervision.

As he sprinkled fresh sprigs of parsley over the fulminating broth, Maurice felt a chin rest on his shoulder – accompanied by a disagreeable odor.

"You make a stew *con pollo?*"

Maurice stepped out from under Mocoso's chin. With dainty swipes of a napkin, he dusted Mocoso's dandruff off his Armani shirt. "*Coq au vin,* my good man."

"Smells *delicioso. Tenémos muy hambre.*"

Good heavens. Surely they didn't expect him to prepare dinner for them as well.

"It appears we may have come to rest on the horns of a dilemma. I was under the assumption that we would make our own victuals. I merely took the initiative to employ the kitchen facilities first. In the matter of a few minutes you'll have the opportunity to explore your own culinary preferences."

Mocoso stared at him for several seconds. "Ah, *sí.*" He called to his partners, "Come *muchachos.* It is time to eat!"

Lorenzo and Rizoso sprang from the couch and scrambled toward the kitchenette, knocking over two chairs and breaking a floor lamp. Mocoso pulled three bowls from a shelf above the sink and divided the contents of the skillet into each. They tipped the bowls to their lips and swilled the *coq au vin.* Maurice drew a breath to protest, but before he could utter a sound, it was all over. What remained on their chins they wiped on filthy sleeves.

With stealth, Maurice placed a palm over an opened tin of beluga caviar – but not quickly enough. Rizoso snatched the tin from the counter, raising the caviar to show his friends.

"For desert, blueberries!" He dipped two fingers splinted with duct tape into the container. Before the others could do the same, Riziso spat the caviar on the floor.

Maurice lunged to save the remainder of the tin, but Rizoso held up a hand to stop him. "No, *señor*. She is spoiled. You must not eat this." And he tossed the can out the screenless window above the sink.

Backing into one of the chairs that still stood upright, Maurice considered a second alternative for his own dinner. But could he muster the alacrity before the others ate it? Then he felt someone's eyes on him.

"*Señor*, you did not get to eat?" Mocoso asked. He swung his fist at Lorenzo and kicked Rizoso. "*Perros*, you ate all his food!"

"*Eey!*" whined Lorenzo. "You ate it, too!"

"*Silencio!*" Mocoso barked. To Maurice he said, "Now we cook for you."

"No, no! Quite alright."

Mocoso shoved his two underlings toward the corner kitchenette, shouting orders at them.

In the meantime, Maurice surrendered any hope of escape and trundled over to the couch. He only hoped he could survive the tribulations of cohabiting with these hooligans for another three or four days. Mr. O'Grady had assured him that the excavation could commence the day after tomorrow. Perhaps the work would progress with haste.

Alas, he would have to endure the unendurable for the sake of the game. These three fools would serve his purposes with their menial labor. And their impact on Pleasance might prove valuable, even diverting. He chuckled to himself. If only he could arrange to be present the first time she encountered them. Poor girl. She hardly recognized the meaningful apprenticeship he'd offered her through their numerous occasions of interaction.

"Here it is, *señor*. We make you a dinner *grande!*" Mocoso beamed as he handed Maurice a bowl and a spoon. Lorenzo and Rizoso stood one step behind, smiling with pride. Maurice looked down at the bowl, where a mound of beans swam in runny ketchup.

* * *

Two bottles of tequila later, the decibel level in the small cabin had quite reached intolerable limits. Mocoso perched backwards on a chair staring at a television as he listened to blaring voices who identified themselves as Marshal Dillon and Miss Kitty. Even so, the dithering western banter from the television speaker did little to mask the cadenced bounce of an old baseball that Lorenzo repeatedly smacked against the wall. Several times he missed catching it, and it thunked the snoring Rizoso on the head – the concussive blows unable to rouse him from an alcoholic stupor on the couch.

Maurice cast a longing look out the window for any signs of Mr. O'Grady's pickup. He and Leona had driven away two hours earlier. Once they returned, Maurice was sure they'd put a stop to the raucous activity in the bunkhouse.

At the shout of "ride 'im, cowboy!" from the television, Mocoso jumped from his chair and pointed at the screen. "Look, *amigos*. They ride wild horses. This is what we must do!"

Lorenzo stopped his game of catch and ran over to watch the television rodeo. "*Sí! Sí!* We will become great *caballeros*. But where will we find horses?"

Mocoso swung his fist against Lorenzo's head. "*Idiota*. This is a ranch. There will be horses. Wake up Rizoso. We go now!"

Maurice cleared his throat. "Might I interject?" He pulled his walker closer. "Such a risky venture might be ill-advised so close to the excavation."

"Come, *viejo*. We will teach you the ways of the horse." Mocoso hooked a hand under Maurice's armpit and guided him toward the door. At the same time, Lorenzo rolled Rizoso off the couch but couldn't rouse the sleeping drunk.

"Leave him," Mocoso said.

Lorenzo reached under Maurice's other armpit, and the two *caballeros* lifted him out the door and down the steps.

"I must object!" Maurice protested. "Our host hasn't given us permission to –"

"Look! A horse," Lorenzo said, pointing to the nearby corral.

The targeted steed ruminated over a manger of hay. It cocked an ear in their direction at their approach. And stopped chewing.

They propped Maurice against the fence and turned to admire the animal.

Something akin to sympathy welled up inside Maurice as he appraised the decrepit beast. Gray hairs peppering the muzzle feathered into a ragged and copper-colored coat. Knobby-kneed legs seemed barely sufficient even to carry the animal's own weight, and a thin veneer of skin scarcely covered a jumble of protruding bones.

"*Magnifico!*" said Mocoso. "Now we will ride."

He and Lorenzo crawled through the rails.

And that's when Maurice noticed certain changes start to come over the horse. A swishing tail. An evil eye?

* * *

Grady backed the truck away from the curb in front of the Lazy S café.

Chewing on a toothpick, he turned to Leona. "Their pie ain't near as good as yours."

"Oh, I don't know about that." She smoothed the dress over her knees and smiled.

Grady knew she appreciated his remark.

He continued down Main Street, a post-meal contentment settling over him. He tried to put out of his mind the next few days' excavation, an interruption to his ranching operation. He should be getting ready to separate those little beefalo calves from their mamas. The markets looked good this year, better than for beef, which was Grady's good luck. Luck that his new neighbor's buffalo bull had broken into his heifer pasture. Luck that the bull had bred all those young cows, and luck that those calves were born hardy critters with more pounds on the hoof.

When that first little beefalo hit the ground the spring before last, he stood faster and suckled sooner than any calf Grady had ever seen. Good thing, too, since March dumped more snow than usual that year. Even the coyotes didn't bother those youngsters – maybe because they were bigger and a little meaner than Angus calves. Hell, he could vouch for that. Branding took several more hands to herd them to the chutes, and once inside, they fought like sons-of-bitches. Even Ole Moss didn't know what to think of them. That crazy old mare didn't like their looks or their smell. Maybe she'd met her match in pure cantankerousness.

Grady shook his head and laughed quietly to himself. He'd never have considered switching from beef if it hadn't happened by mistake. Yeah, he was pissed when Chantale's bull tore down the fence, but he sure didn't cry when he sold that first crop of beefalo babies. Now, several other ranchers in the valley planned on doing the same.

Funny how things sometimes worked out.

"Slow down. There's some people in the road up there," Leona warned.

Grady pressed his foot against the break and brought the pickup to a standstill as Carl stood in the center lane and stopped traffic. Two men dragged a barricade across the street right in front of him. The rancher rolled his window down as the sheriff sauntered over.

"Evening, Grady. Leona," the sheriff said, leaning over to prop an elbow on the open window. "We're blocking Main for a couple of hours and setting up a detour."

"What's going on?" Grady asked.

"That movie company's going to be shooting a scene in a little while. You're free to watch here, if you want."

Grady turned to Leona.

She shrugged. "Up to you."

About that time, two vans passed Grady and parked on the other side of the barricade. The sliding doors opened and out jumped a group of actors, Grady supposed, since they were dressed like aliens. He'd heard they were making a spaceman movie in town.

"Naw," he said to Carl. "I'll just turn around."

"If you come back to town tomorrow, stay clear of Main. They're filming here again most of the day."

He nodded goodbye to the sheriff and cranked the wheel of the pickup. As he continued back the way he'd come, he met two more vans with logos on the side that read, "*Silverville vs. the Flying Saucers.*" And handfuls of townspeople walked towards the filming site.

"This is foolishness," Grady mumbled, and he gripped the steering wheel harder.

"They'll be gone soon enough."

"Not for me."

What the hell had happened to this town? Folks here used to be normal, hardworking people who didn't put up with crazy nonsense like this. That boy Howard thinking he saw a UFO started all kinds of shenanigans, bringing all sorts of odd folks to town. Why, he himself had seen a UFO at the Labor Day celebration two years ago, but it didn't turn *him* into a crackpot. And people claimed Silverville sat on – what were they, ley lines? Anyway, something that caused all manner of havoc. Hogwash was what it was. Well, okay, there was the curse, but those Conquistadors might have left curses all over the country.

"Indigestion?" Leona asked.

"Huh?"

"Well, you're scowling like something's not sitting well."

"It ain't."

* * *

"What's going on over at Ole Moss's corral?" Leona asked, as Grady parked the pickup in front of the house.

He squinted through the last rays of sun toward the barns and corral. Two of the fellows he'd just hired to dig staggered inside the fence, drunk, hands raised in front of them as they approached Ole Moss. Maurice leaned against the rails, motioning with his arms to get Grady's attention.

What the hell were they doing in that pen? Nobody had given them permission to bother his stock. He stomped toward the corral.

"Thank Providence for your timely arrival!" Maurice said. "I admonished them for this foolhardy act, but they appear determined to mount your steed."

Grady picked up a pitchfork, ready to send those boys scattering. Then he noticed the old mare staring back at the two drunks, fire in her eyes, tail flicking with anticipation. He paused, stroked the stubble on his chin, and reappraised the situation. Maybe he wouldn't chase them out after all. Maybe he'd let Ole Moss teach them a lesson herself.

He rolled a bale of hay closer to the fence and sat down. He twisted around and called back to his wife, who still stood beside the pickup. "Leona, come on over here, and bring a couple beers."

"You must accept my apologies," Maurice said. "I was ineffectual in stopping them."

"Ain't worried. Ole Moss can take care of herself."

Inside the corral, Lorenzo tiptoed to the mare's side and leaned over to get hold of her mane. She stepped sideways just out of reach. Again, he tried the same thing and the horse cocked a back leg at the unsuspecting man. Grady guffawed, knowing full well the warning signs to keep away.

The third time Lorenzo approached, Ole Moss not only cocked a leg but kicked out in his direction, popping him in the kneecap. He dropped to the ground with a yelp, and doubled over to grip his knee.

"*Aye! Chihuahua!* What spirit this fine stallion shows," Mocoso said, stepping over Lorenzo.

At that, Grady laughed out loud.

Mocoso turned and shouted, "*Señor*, watch as we tame this horse for you."

"I'm watchin'."

Leona walked up with the beers and sat down on the bale next to Grady. "You're not going to let them try that, are you?"

"Maybe for a little while." He popped the tab on the can and took a swig.

Mocoso pulled Lorenzo to his feet and motioned for him to circle around to the other side of the mare. "Come and hold him tight while I get on."

Lorenzo walked a wide sweep around the back of Ole Moss and cautiously sidled up to the horse. He wrapped his arms around her neck, taking a handful of mane in his fingers.

Mocoso picked up a bucket and dropped it upside down next to the horse's shoulder. He placed his left hand on her withers, stepped up on the bucket, and slid onto her back.

Ole Moss didn't move.

Leona asked, "Why's she just standing there?"

"Just wait," Grady said, and raised the beer to his mouth. But just then, Mocoso kicked Ole Moss in the ribs. Grady paused.

The horse continued to stand perfectly still, and Mocoso kicked her again. This time, she flattened her ears and snorted. Grady set the can between his knees. "Here it comes." Almost in slow motion, the old horse reared on her back legs, standing motionless for a second or two and dangling Lorenzo from her mane. Quick as a bobcat springing on a packrat, she lunged forward, tucking her head between her front legs and kicking her back legs high in the air. Mocoso sailed over her head like a rock launched from a catapult. Before he could hit the ground, she spun and clipped him with both hooves while his body flew through the air. The force of the kick propelled him into the barn wall, and he sank to the ground.

Still hugging the horse's neck, Lorenzo screamed. Ole Moss spun on her hind legs, circle after circle. All that Grady could see was the bottoms of his boots with each revolution.

"Why don't that boy let go?"

"Grady, I think his hands are caught in the mane," Leona replied.

Grady took another swig of beer. "Yeah, you may be right."

At that moment, Lorenzo's hands broke free and his body crashed into the rails.

Ole Moss stopped, dropped her head, and ambled toward the manger to finish her supper.

Grady stood from the bale. "Good thing you boys got one more day before we start digging."

"You just gonna leave them there?" Leona asked, following him back to the house.

"Reckon so. Ole Moss looks fine to me."

* * *

"Hand me that smallest wrench on the shelf," Perry said, tightening the vise around a strut of the unicycle's frame.

Pleasance scanned rows of shelves situated above layers of boxes that lined the garage wall. "And where would this wrench be?"

"Oh, sorry. Red toolbox on the first shelf."

She found the tool and handed it to him. "There sure are a lot of boxes in here, Uncle Perry."

"Yep. Lots of memories."

While he spun the wheel, checking for wobble, Pleasance moved over to the closest box and opened the flaps. Scuba goggles stared back at her. Beside them, large rubber flippers draped over a metal oxygen tank. She rummaged in the box until she found the regulator. "Oh, I remember when we last used this stuff."

Perry looked up. "Remember the trouble we got into with the Sudanese authorities?"

"Not as well as you do!"

They both snorted a laugh.

Perry had taken the family on one of his adventure vacations – this one off the west coast of the Red Sea. They'd bare-boat rented a schooner, which Perry had stocked with winches, ropes, and enough scuba gear to outfit a team of Navy SEALS. Evenings on the schooner, they'd pored over maps that marked sunken vessels submerged for centuries. But Perry had bought one map from an antiquities dealer on the streets of Johannesburg that particularly interested him. It detailed the location of a wreck about nine nautical miles from the ancient trading port of Berenike. For a week, they searched the sandy shallows of the sea floor, looking for any sign of the sunken first-century Roman vessel. Perry, of course, found the first pieces of the broken mast, and summoned the others to join him in the underwater excavation. After two days, the crew tallied several broken wine-storage amphoras, a nearly perfect ivory sculpture, and a salt-corroded mechanism filled with cogs and gears.

On the third day, they surfaced to find themselves surrounded by three coastal gunboats. Fortunately, not pirates, but instead local authorities, who apprehended the whole family and escorted them to Port Sudan. The police confiscated the entire cache of recovered booty and released everyone – except for Perry, whom they arrested and jailed.

Pleasance wouldn't stand for it. While the rest of the family dealt with the American consulate, she headed for the nearest liquor store and bought a bottle of whiskey. The guy behind the counter never even asked for an ID. At only fourteen, she could already pass for twenty-six.

Then she went to the police station and waited outside until late evening. When she felt certain that most of the guards had left, she marched into the building and demanded to see Uncle Perry. The two night-shift guards laughed at her until she produced the bottle. They brought out three glasses and poured, apparently expecting her to join them. Pleasance had never tasted anything stronger than a sip of wine at family gatherings, but she managed to nurse the whiskey until the guards became drunk and fell asleep. She sacked the desk and found the keys, carrying them into the next room, where Perry sat in a cell.

"I'm here to spring you!" she announced.

But instead of showing appreciation, Perry shook his head. "You can't just break me out of here. I don't want Interpol on my tail the rest of my life. Your Aunt Paula will take care of this, uh, misunderstanding."

Perry forced her to replace the keys and return to the hotel. Two days later, Aunt Paula did, indeed, manage to get Perry out. No one ever told Pleasance how much it cost, but the bribe was considerably more than a bottle of whiskey.

Now squatting on the floor of her uncle's garage, Pleasance replaced the regulator in the box and closed the flap. While Perry continued to tinker with the unicycle, she wrestled the carton back against the wall, noticing a large plaque squeezed between a spelunking helmet and a Maasai spear. She lifted the plaque and showed it to Perry.

"What's this?"

"Family coat of arms."

She peered at the complex engravings on the shield. They consisted of the obligatory wreaths and banners, the words "Pantiwycke" decorating the bottom in ornate Old English lettering. In the center, a prancing lion held a severed head in its mouth.

"What's with the lion and the head?"

"Great-great-great Grandpa Profundius did some very bad things. Don't ask."

Perry didn't give Pleasance time to pose another question. He pulled the unicycle out of the vise and bounced it on the floor. "Sure you wanna ride this old thing?"

"Hey, I need the exercise. Sitting at a phone all day is making my thighs big."

Perry handed her the cycle.

"Well, not now. Maybe tomorrow." Pleasance looked at her watch. "You getting hungry? I wonder what Aunt Lela has made for dinner."

"She's not here. We'll have to order out."

"Aunt Lela is never here anymore. Where is she all the time?"

Perry shrugged and walked over to the garage door. "I suppose she's out playing with her chicken fanatic friends."

* * *

Howard checked the clock on the wall – 8:15 p.m. Visiting hours were supposed to be over at eight o'clock. That's when Mr. Fine had told him to lock the doors, but when Mrs. O'Cleary had walked in just at closing time, he couldn't tell her to leave. She signed the guest book in the room where her deceased neighbor, Mr. Thomas, was lying in state, and eventually returned to the reception room to tell Howard about her meditation group and how he should join them.

"You'd find the whole experience relaxing, Howard. The hardest thing is learning how to clear your thoughts and empty your mind."

Howard had nodded politely and thanked her for coming. He didn't tell her so, but he didn't think he would go to the meditation group. He might already know how to meditate if that meant clearing your thoughts. Just sitting at the funeral home waiting for people to come in gave him plenty of time to sit with an empty mind. It was one of the things he liked best about working for Mr. Fine. There was always lots of time to sit. And he liked to greet and offer cookies to the people who came into the funeral home. Of course, they were there to pay their respects, but dead people couldn't speak. It was up to Howard to do that for them.

"How do you do, Mrs. So-n-So. Would you like a cookie? I'm sure Mr. Such-n-Such appreciates that you came to see him." He would smile. She would smile. Everybody whispered, and it was all very soothing.

Howard locked the front door and turned off the lights in the reception room. He walked through the building, turning off lamps, making sure everything was in its place. Since Mr. Thomas's service was the next morning, Mr. Fine had asked Howard to vacuum the chapel before he went home that night. He opened the closet and pulled out the Hoover, uncoiling the cord to the floor.

Just as he was about to start, the buzzer from the garage door sounded. He wondered who it could be since visitors usually came to the front door. Maybe a late delivery from the florist. He walked down the hall, through the embalming room, and into the garage, where he pushed the automatic door opener button.

As the garage door slowly rose, the silhouettes of four figures stood backlit by the outside security lamp. Their heads and bodies appeared square to Howard, so he flipped on the garage lights to get a better look.

What he saw made him jump backwards. Four spacemen stared back at him. He knew they were spacemen because their heads were covered in brown helmets, silver antennas poking upwards. And their robes showed pictures of stars and moons – except one, which was covered in yellow flowers.

"Welcome, Spacemen," Howard said. He figured they might contact him again after that first time almost four years ago. He'd been riding his bike home from work at the funeral home late one night. In the woods beside the road a red glow shimmered through the trees. At first, Howard thought that it was a fire, but after getting closer, he saw a triangular set of lights hovering above the ground and humming. He didn't know how long he stood there. Maybe five minutes. And just like that, it floated upwards and disappeared.

And now they were back.

One of the aliens took a step forward and held out a small black box. "Earthling, we come in peace," the communicator box said. "We have a message for you."

I knew it. I knew it, he thought. He'd always felt they had a message for him. And that's why they were here now. "Would you like a cookie?"

A voice came from the box again. "Do not be afraid, Earthling."

"I'm not afraid. I know you won't hurt me."

"We will not hurt you." The alien took the communicator box in both hands and pressed a button. Howard heard a high-pitched squealing sound. The communicator must not be working right.

"What is your message?"

The voice of the box said, "Earthling, we come in peace. We have a message for you."

The aliens started looking at each other. The alien in the flower robe stepped next to the alien with the box and took it away. "Howard," it said in a funny voice that sounded a little like Russian, "just take this note to Mayor Earl Bob Jackson tonight."

"Okay."

The alien handed Howard an envelope. The four slowly backed away, turned and ran into the parking lot. They jumped into a car and sped away.

He wondered why the aliens were using a car, but he decided they had to get back to their spacecraft somehow.

He turned the sealed envelope over in his hands, expecting to see some strange symbols or writing, but it was blank.

He would take the alien message right to Mr. Jackson. But first he would finish vacuuming and then get a cookie.

* * *

Pleasance navigated the unicycle through the garage door and headed downtown. A little shaky at first, but it only took a few blocks for her to regain a feel for the balance of riding on one wheel. Uncle Perry had taught her how to ride when she'd decided at the age of ten she wanted to be a circus performer. On weekends, he'd indulged her childhood fantasy by constructing a series of obstacle courses that ran the length of the parking lot of his veterinary supply company. She soon became adept at ascending ramps, jumping through hoops, and carving tight serpentine arcs around boxes of syringes and equine speculums.

Ah, yes, it was all coming back to her. She tried a few gutter jumps, her metal toe clips helping to keep her airborne.

Up ahead, a flowered tent lumbered along the sidewalk. As she drew closer she recognized Madame Pompeii's generous backside.

"Heads up, Aunt Penny! I'm right behind you."

Madame Pompeii stopped and turned around to look at her, clutching a hand to her chest. "Oh my goodness!"

Pleasance circled the woman twice to bleed off her momentum until she was barely rolling. She maneuvered the unicycle back and forth, airplaning her arms to keep her balance. "Where you headed?"

"Downtown to the Farmer's Market. They've blocked off a side street next to Main. I'm looking for some fresh mugwort. You don't suppose they'll have any, do you?"

"No idea. Well, maybe I'll see you down there." Pleasance pushed against the pedals and shot forward.

Main Street would be a busy place today. Besides the Farmer's Market and usual summer sidewalk sales on one end, the film company would be shooting on the other end according to Uncle Perry.

As she neared downtown, she could see people milling about tables set up just outside the storefronts. She veered into the throngs, barely missing a child holding an ice-cream cone.

"Hey, watch out!" a woman next to the child scolded her. "You're not supposed to ride on the sidewalks."

"Oh, sorry." Pleasance hopped off the unicycle and rolled it alongside her toward a group of tables in front of the sporting goods store. She bypassed the women's clothing – too frilly and hardly durable enough for her level of activity – and stopped at a stack of men's hiking pants. She picked up a pair with cargo pockets and zip-off legs. She slung them over her shoulder and steered the unicycle into the store to try them on. Even men's trousers didn't always accommodate the girth of her thighs. But the long line at the dressing room looked discouraging, so she draped the pants over a shirt rack and squeezed back out of the store. Maybe she'd try them on later.

She rolled her wheel past a couple of shops and stopped again at a table filled with binoculars, spotting scopes, lamps welded from horseshoes, and ashtrays shaped like flying saucers.

"Welcome to Price's Gun Paradise, little lady."

It was the man she'd try to avoid while standing in the queue for that film crew job.

"Hey, I know you," he said.

Great. She pushed the unicycle between them to block him from getting any closer. "I don't think so."

"Of course I do. I never forget a face – especially one like yours." His jowls spread to display a row of yellow teeth. "You been to that theme park yet?"

"Not yet."

"It'd be my pleasure to escort you around. I could even get you a discount rate on a ticket. What do you say?"

At that moment, a man stepped between them and asked about the price on a laser bore-sighting kit. Pleasance took the opportunity to duck away. She stepped off the curb, mounted her unicycle, and pedaled towards the Farmer's Market.

Two blocks further down, she spotted on a side street a cluster of open-sided tents filled with people selling bakery goods, produce, and artwork. She again hopped off her cycle and wandered around the stalls.

Two vendors away, Madame Pompeii stood arguing over the price of a lava lamp. Her aunt appeared to notice her and motioned to come over, but Pleasance pretended not to see, turning the other direction.

And came face-to-face with Mocoso and his two sidekicks.

CHAPTER TEN

Madame Pompeii looked where Pleasance had been standing, but the girl had disappeared. She turned back to the vendor, shaking the lava lamp in his face.

"I could buy one of these at the Shop-Mart for a fraction of the price you're asking."

"Good luck," the artisan said. "You won't even find one of these at Shop-Mart. This lamp is a handmade one-of-a-kind."

She turned the lamp one way and another, watching the lava globs float like disconnected faces in her crystal ball. "Will you take twenty-five dollars then?"

The artisan frowned and appeared to be thinking. "Well, how about twenty-seven fifty?"

Madame Pompeii set the lamp down and reached into her purse. But sudden shouts from the other side of the market distracted her. In the chaos of people jumping aside, she saw Pleasance escaping with haste on that ridiculous unicycle of Perry's. To her surprise, the three Latin men she'd seen in her crystal ball chased close behind. Madame Pompeii clucked in dismay. Why would Pleasance go to such great lengths just to avoid relationships? She'd somehow driven off that nice young Italian man, and now she was trying to ditch these fellows. They were obviously interested in her – the crystal ball said so. There was such a thing as playing too hard to get.

She fished around in her purse for the money to pay for the lamp. After she'd counted out the bills and change, she claimed her new purchase and walked in the direction of the film shoot a block away.

In her opinion, Perry had always influenced that girl too much, nurturing her independent and wild nature. Too bad he had lived so close to Pleasance's family, making it all too easy to insinuate himself into her life. Sometimes, Madame Pompeii felt that she should have intervened, providing a more stable role model for the girl.

"Excuse me," said a voice in a strong Texan drawl. "Would ya'll like to sign this petition?" The woman who blocked her way wore a skintight body suit, heavy western belt, and ostrich cowboy boots. Madame Pompeii recognized her at once. Chantale, from the journeying session. Beside her towered Hans High Horse, appearing very thin and white with a long ponytail. His outfit matched the woman's. He thrust forward a clipboard and pencil.

"What's this about?" Madame Pompeii asked.

Chantale answered, "It's to put a stop to animal husbandry."

"The unnatural joining of any man to one of Wapa Wapa's wild creatures," chimed in the pale companion, "is an abomination."

"Wapa what?"

"Wapa Wapa, the great spirit who binds the universe together, making all things possible, all things magnificent and holy."

Madame Pompeii looked back to the woman. "What's he talking about?"

"He's talking about the unholy practice of people making animals husbands."

"That's legal?"

"Not in the eyes of Wapa Wapa," the man crooned.

Chantale added, "You ask if animal husbandry is legal? Why darlin', they even have classes for it at Texas Tech. Hans, give her the petition."

Madame Pompeii handed Hans the lava lamp and took the petition: *We the guardians of God's noble creatures demand that the practice of Animal Husbandry be banned for the immorality that it is.*

There were two signatures on the petition: Chantale's and that of Hans High Horse. Madame Pompeii scribbled her own name underneath, retrieved the lava lamp, and scurried on her way.

By the time she reached the film shoot, a crowd of spectators had already gathered. The excitement was absolutely contagious, and she wondered what kinds of interesting things she would see that day.

* * *

Pleasance swung the unicycle like a bat at her three assailants, catching one on the side of the head. That made the other two pause just long enough for her to take a running jump onto her wheel for a getaway. Not an easy task since she had to weave around people, leashed dogs, and vendor tents. She sure could have used a little help from Cap. But he was gone.

She took a quick glance over her shoulder, only to see the three men closing in. Veering toward a produce stand, she shouted and waved her arms at shoppers, "Get out of the way!"

People froze in surprise and she nearly knocked down those closest to the tent. But she still managed to blitz between them and the table to snatch up a watermelon, which she lobbed over her head, hoping to hit one of her pursuers – or at least to cause enough chaos to slow them down. She never looked back to see if her plan worked. Instead, she pedaled straight down Main Street, following the center line between foot traffic.

Son tres necios! The Three Fools! That's what Tomás had called them. So they *were* in Silverville when they called her at work. Were they toying with her? No, they weren't smart enough to know she answered a phone at Telemarketing Enterprises.

They had to be after that jade mask. But she *hadn't* stolen it – Maurice had. Should she stop the chase right now and give them Maurice's address in New York? No, they wouldn't believe her. And considering what they did to Tomás, she'd better keep running.

She glanced to the side and saw the alcove entrance of a micro-brew pub. Perhaps they wouldn't notice if she ducked inside. She wheeled off the street and into the alcove, stopping just long enough to peer around the wall corner. Mocoso and his friends ran – or rather, limped – down the sidewalk toward her. One of them pointed directly at the spot where she stood.

Now she had to make a decision. Either barrel out of the alcove and down the street, or turn into the pub, making a dash for the back patio and into the alley. They were too close. She opened the door and hopped back on the unicycle. But she had forgotten the sunken floor plan. The wheel bounced down four steps into the establishment and collided with a bar stool, which her outstretched hand sent spinning. Patrons looked up in shock as she tore down the aisle, making a beeline for the patio. There was no chance to avoid the waiter who rounded the bar, carrying a tray of full mugs, and she knocked him to the floor in a puddle of broken glass and beer. By the time she was out the back door, she heard the three black marketeers tumbling down the steps behind her.

Luckily, few customers sat in the patio, making it easy to maneuver around the tables to the alley entrance. But once there, she nearly slammed into a garbage truck, blocking the road to her right. She cut to the left instead and pumped hard, flying out of the alley and onto a cross street, where she turned right. A half block further, Pleasance jumped the curb and found herself in the city's public playground. Still, the men remained close behind. Realizing too late that she had ridden into a bed of wood chips that slowed her almost to a stop, she dismounted and began to run, carrying the unicycle with her. She ducked through the monkey bars and around the merry-go-round to reach the street again. With a flying leap, she landed back on the cycle and looked behind. Mocoso and Lorenzo were lifting kids' bikes lying on the grass; Rizoso was already kick-pedaling a stolen scooter in her direction. Within minutes, they began to close the gap.

Pleasance decided to turn at the next intersection back toward Main Street in the hope of losing or slowing them down in the heavy foot traffic. At the crossroad, she veered right toward the largest crowd. The film shoot. Maybe she could ditch them in that throng.

* * *

Madame Pompeii joined the crowd at the film shoot and craned her neck around the heads in front of her to watch. Someone had placed pieces of tape on the pavement and actors dressed in gray neoprene suits and hideous headgear paced over to the marks in front of the "spaceship" parked on Main Street. Only the camera side of the craft looked real; the back was open and consisted of a skeletal frame of two-by-fours and wire mesh. The curved surface of the saucer that she could see from her vantage point shone with some type of metallic material. A relay of lights flashed in a repeated sequence around the shiny exterior.

A man sitting in a chair labeled "Director" held a megaphone. "Okay, people, let's get this scene rolling! Aliens, take your places on the ramp behind the spaceship door. Soldiers, get on your marks."

The film company's security crew herded the crowd of spectators back beyond the camera's angle of view. The actors trotted toward the spaceship and disappeared around the back.

"Quiet on the set! Camera! And ... action!"

The camera trained on the spacecraft and, slowly, the hatch opened, dropping a ramp to the concrete sidewalk. Three aliens appeared through the doorway, each one holding a futuristic weapon. At the same time, the soldiers lined up in a semicircle firing position around the craft. The aliens walked down the ramp and faced the troops.

"Surrender now, Earthmen, or face total annihilation!"

The captain of the soldiers shouted at his men, "Ready, aim, ..."

The defenders of Earth had no time to fire a shot. The aliens raised their weapons and lurched back as though their guns had discharged a powerful force.

The soldiers clutched their chests and fell to the ground, rolling and moaning in pain.

Madame Pompeii whispered to the kid next to her. "What killed them? I didn't see or hear anything."

The kid rolled his eyes. "Duh! They'll add that stuff with special effects later."

"Oh, of course." She nodded knowingly.

At that moment, Pleasance on her unicycle burst through the spacecraft door, taking flight a good ten feet above the ramp. She smashed into the alien leader, knocking him over like a bowling pin. She hit the pavement and tumbled forward in a tight roll, her ride skidding along beside her. Springing to her feet, she grabbed the cycle and turned to face the hatch door. Within seconds, two men on bicycles launched through the door, also flying over the ramp. They managed to mow down the remaining aliens before crashing. Pleasance swung the unicycle at the first bicyclist as he tried to stand and sent him sprawling to the ground. As the other one ran towards her, she grabbed his hair, dropped to her knees, and used his momentum to fling him over her shoulders. She leaped back on her unicycle and pedaled straight toward the director's chair. He threw his arms up before his face, bracing for impact, but Pleasance bounced the unicycle in the air, grabbed the camera crane scaffold above his head with both hands, and cleared the chair by several feet.

People screamed and divided to either side as Pleasance tore through the crowd, the two men now chasing her on foot. Shocked silence settled over the set, and everyone turned to look at a third man on a child's scooter, who kick-pedaled around the spacecraft, past the fallen aliens, around the director, and in the direction of the chase.

The director stood and retrieved the dropped megaphone. "Who were those people? I want to know that woman's name!"

A man standing nearby in the crowd said, "I want to know the same thing."

Madame Pompeii gasped when she noticed the gold ring in his bottom lip. The same unsettling figure she'd seen in her dream.

* * *

A knock came at the bunkhouse a little after sunrise, but Maurice was already up and dressed. All three of his roommates still slept, snoring at softer decibels than they had throughout the night. The evening before, they had arrived at the bunkhouse in their own vehicle, which Mr. O'Grady had repaired earlier that day. They had staggered into the room grumbling about an encounter with a certain "*mujer más grande*."

By the looks of their disheveled appearance and mangled bodies, he surmised their remark referred to Pleasance. Most endearing. His young protégé must have proven more than a match for them. She escaped, of course, much to their dismay.

A second knock, more insistent, came from the door.

Maurice clutched his walker and ambled to the entranceway. He opened the door to Mr. O'Grady, who jerked a thumb over his shoulder toward the running pickup. "Time to let them boys start earning their keep."

"I'm afraid you've come before they have had a chance to awaken."

"Get 'em up. Time's a wastin'." Mr. O'Grady walked back down the steps toward the pickup.

"Are we to start the excavation this morning?"

"Nope, just clearing the mouth of the cave. Today, anyway."

"Tomorrow then."

"Maybe. Depends on how high the water table got in that cave." Mr. O'Grady opened the door to the pickup and laid on the horn.

A cacophonous scuffling filled the room behind Maurice as the three laborers scrambled to their feet. Still in their clothes from the previous night, they filed past him and out the door.

"If you'll give me a moment," Maurice called out, "I'll retrieve my jacket."

The rancher climbed in the cab and shut the pickup door. Through the open window, he said, "No sense in you coming today."

By that time the digging crew had arranged themselves in the bed of the truck. Maurice had no opportunity to object by the time Mr. O'Grady pulled away from the bunkhouse.

No matter. Maurice would participate in the opening whether invited or not. But at a discreet distance.

He offered a cheerful wave to his bunkmates. *"Bonne continuation, mes amis!"* He chuckled to himself. They couldn't possibly perform at optimum efficiency in their current piteous condition. The thrashing they had received by Pleasance, coupled with their constant affinity for insobriety, simply would not permit it.

Ah, a relaxing day in the countryside observing the honest sweat of others. While he hummed a strain from Mendelssohn's "May Breezes," Maurice began to think about the items he would require for the outing. He cleared the kitchen table so it could serve to organize his inventory. On the first row, he placed the spotting scope, sanitary wipes, insect repellant, and parasol. These he would store in his surveillance rucksack. On the second row – all destined for a picnic basket – he assembled a wedge of fine-aged cheese, imported olives from Tuscany, a fresh baguette, a bottle of Chauvignon blanc (too hot outside for Merlot), and matching tablecloth and napkins. Beside these he added his iPod, freshly downloaded with Purcell's *Dido and Aeneus*, Act III, the final scene, and a worn volume from Proust's *À la recherche du temps perdu*.

He stood back to survey his collection. Cocking his head to one side, he stared at the sanitary wipes. No, they didn't belong in the rucksack. He moved them to the lower row. But what of the iPod and book? Perhaps too cumbersome for the basket. These items he slid to the first row.

Once again, he stood back to assess the arrangement. Perfect.

With great care, Maurice packed the rucksack items first, handling each one like a fragile China doll. He repeated the same ritual for the picnic basket.

But plenty of time for a cup of tea before he started his day of long-range supervision. He filled a pot of water and placed it on the stove. Reaching for a tin of Earl Grey tea from the cupboard, Maurice measured out precisely two-and-half teaspoons into a steeper and dropped it into the water. He waited exactly four minutes to allow the water to reach the correct temperature. After an appropriate interval of time, he poured tea into a cup and savored the aroma. A sip. Delicious. Perhaps he would present Mrs. O'Grady with the remainder of the tin to better civilize the barbarity of her lifestyle on the ranch. His small token could allow her to discard that reviling Lipton tea.

He finished his cup, slipped on an unlined flak jacket, and spritzed two squirts of Polo Sport on his lapel from his cologne atomizer. Two trips to the SUV later, he climbed into the driver's seat and started the engine. He began to follow the tracks that Mr. O'Grady's truck had carved into the soft road behind the ranch.

* * *

Every morning for the past several days, Pleasance's routine had begun with a trip to the hill above Grady's ranch. The only way to discover the whereabouts of the Spanish treasure would be to keep a tight surveillance on the old rancher's activity. Perry had told her that it was just a matter of days before the ground dried up enough for Grady to start the excavation. Well, it had been a few days, and she still hadn't observed any sign of him doing anything other than regular ranch work.

This morning, however, the routine seemed different. Grady had loaded his pickup with shovels and driven behind the barn, out of sight from her vantage point on the hill. After a few minutes, the truck reappeared, three men sitting in the bed, as the vehicle rolled out the driveway. Grady must have picked up some grunts to do the heavy work. Probably let them stay in the bunkhouse which, she remembered, sat behind the barn.

No time to waste. Pleasance ran back to her car and flipped open her cell phone to call Pat Montgomery, telling him she wouldn't get to work until that afternoon. She waited for the pickup to pass below her. When Grady had driven a half mile down the road past the hill, she eased her car out behind him, careful to follow at a safe distance. Even though the rains had just stopped a few days ago, the gravel already spewed dust from Grady's wheels. The trip took Pleasance past a large sandstone outcropping and beside a small grove of dead evergreen trees. The path became rough and uneven with football-sized boulders strewn across the width of the single lane. Here the road narrowed and dropped into a ravine before straightening out onto a flat, where the jeep trail completely played out. Fearing that they could see her, she had to slow her progress almost to a stop until Grady's pickup bounced over the terrain, rounded a bend, and dropped below another hill. She watched and waited for more dust to spiral above the ridgeline, but there was none. The pickup must have stopped.

She rolled her car forward as close as she could and killed the engine. Clutching her binoculars for the reconnoiter, she wound her way through thick sagebrush, raising her arms as she pushed through the snagging branches. At the same time, her feet slipped off wobbly rocks that threatened to throw her off balance with each upslope stride. The closer she got to the ridgeline the more the vegetation thinned until it became bare terrain.

Pleasance dropped to her hands and knees to stay out of sight as she cleared the summit. In the half light of early morning, she saw Grady and his workers, still only shadows carrying shovels, moving part way up the opposite side of the arroyo below her. Just above them was clearly the mouth of a cave, rockslides and debris covering most of the opening. She climbed partially down the slope to position herself behind a large boulder, close enough to hear their voices.

From the summit behind her, light spilled into the arroyo as the sun peeked over the hill. And that's when she recognized them. The Three Fools.

What were they doing there? Did they follow her and manage to meet Grady? Or had they met him before and somehow made it to Silverville at the same time she was there? Surely, he didn't plan on selling them the artifacts. Did he?

Pleasance set her binoculars down and took a deep breath to slow her heart rate.

Maybe this wasn't the treasure site; maybe this was some other ranch project. But that made no sense. The only reason to dig into a cave in the middle of nowhere was to retrieve something valuable. This had to be the place.

She raised her binoculars back to her eyes and strained to hear their words. Grady pointed at the cave mouth, and The Three Fools hefted their shovels to sink them into loose debris. Partial phrases wafted up the arroyo to her: "… open a hole near the top … as much done as possible … check that water table …"

Grady sat down and leaned against a rock while his accomplices dug.

Knowing the shadow of the hill would hide her until noon, Pleasance made herself as comfortable as possible. She needed to learn their plans before she left. From what she could make out from their conversation, there was water in the cave. And this could pose a problem in recovering the artifacts. But it could also buy her time to formulate her own plan to beat them to the punch.

After an hour, Rizoso sat down and Grady started cursing at him. Mocoso slammed the handle of his shovel against the back of Rizoso's head, the thrust of the impact sending him rolling down the slope. It took ten minutes of arguing for Grady to get them back on the job. Pleasance glanced at her watch. She had maybe one more hour before she had to head into work.

About thirty minutes later, The Three Fools breached the top rocks blocking the cave mouth, and a spume of water began cascading down the hill. Soon, water gushed in torrents toward the arroyo floor as the four men struggled to get clear of the flow. But the current eventually slowed to a trickle. Lorenzo clambered up the pitch to the hole and poked his head inside. The others climbed up and crowded around him. A ruckus erupted from the group as Lorenzo's entire body vanished into the opening. He must have fallen in. Mocoso slid down the slope to the pickup and returned with a rope, one end of which he tossed into the hole. All three men tugged until Lorenzo's head reappeared. They gave one final yank and the fool tumbled out. Dripping and muddy, he struggled to his feet and whooped, raising a hand above his head. He held something gold and shiny.

"This is the place," Pleasance muttered to herself.

The dry men all clustered around him for several seconds. Grady plucked the object from Lorenzo's hand and started shouting.

"This ain't your business. You're being paid to dig."

And, unbelievably, Grady climbed back to the hole and tossed the object through the opening.

"Get back to work, boys! This hole has got to get a lot bigger," he shouted at them again.

And when it does, she thought, *I'm going to get there first. Tonight.*

A breezy gust knocked over her canteen. She leaned forward to retrieve it and straightened back up. Polo Sport. It was on the wind, she could swear it. She sucked in her nostrils trying to catch the scent again, but all she could smell was sage. In a panic, she whirled around on her haunches to survey the ridgeline, expecting to see Maurice behind her. All she saw was a bare hill line and a lone raven circling overhead.

* * *

It had taken a half hour for Maurice to locate the most suitable spot, a high ridgeline that surveyed the entire arroyo and the drama that began playing out beneath him. Center stage were the three obnoxious barbarians, poorly following the orders shouted by Mr. O'Grady. Maurice only hoped their labor would tire them sufficiently for him to enjoy uninterrupted repose that evening.

To stage right, and somewhat above, perched Pleasance behind a boulder peering through binoculars at the haphazard players. She struggled against talus to conceal herself.

A movement several hundred yards below Maurice's position caught his attention. As expected, Mr. Cappelli appeared, as it were, in the wings for an unannounced role in this thespian escapade. Above Pleasance he crouched on a ledge, seeming to take great care to be discreet and unobserved by all the others.

Maurice chuckled as he popped a Tuscany olive into his mouth. Yes, the game had truly developed into a sporting diversion.

* * *

Lela sat with her head in her hands, a glum look on her face. "Well, this is certainly a setback," she said to Denton.

The operation hadn't exactly gone according to plan. They'd sat half the night across the street from City Hall, waiting for the signal that Earl Bob had gotten the note and agreed to their terms for the hostage exchange. But no half-lowered shade had appeared in the north window of the second floor. That was to be the signal that Earl Bob would meet them at a remote campground with the detainees incarcerated in the gym. By three o'clock in the morning, City Hall remained silent and the ATEP team returned home, disappointed that they would have to feed Bob and Arno at least another day. Or worse, Earl Bob had rejected their proposal, and they were back where they started.

Of course, it never occurred to them that Howard hadn't delivered the note.

"Well, he did finally deliver it – just twelve hours after we asked him to," Denton reported.

"What was the hold up?"

"Lela, it's Howard. He changed into sneakers before he left and didn't realize the note was stuck to the bottom of his work shoes." He stood. "More coffee?"

"Yeah, we both need it."

Denton picked up both Fine Funeral Home mugs and walked over to the counter to refill their cups.

Felicia poked her head in the door. "It's the Thomas family. They want to talk to you about what happened during the service this morning."

"Tell them I'll be up there in a minute."

Felicia nodded. "Don't be too long." She stepped back out of the room.

"Problem?" Lela asked.

"Sort of. Howard found the note on the bottom of his shoe during the service. Wouldn't have been a big deal, but he announced it when the minister asked us all to observe a moment of silence for the deceased."

He set the coffee pot back on the counter, talking as he handed Lela her mug. "You should have seen the look on everyone's faces when Howard shouted, 'The aliens gave me a message! I have to deliver it!' Then he ran out the door."

"I'm sorry, Denton. This has been one fiasco after another. But Earl Bob has the message now, right?"

"Yes."

"Do you think he'll show up for the exchange tonight?"

"Hope so. That Arno is really getting on my nerves." He put on his suit coat and started for the door. "Have to cut this short, Lela. Got to put out a fire."

Lela dropped her head back into her hands. She felt so tired from last night, but now it looked like tonight would be a repeat performance. They should have given instructions in the note for Earl Bob to drop the shade no later than ten o'clock. Now, they would just have to sit and watch until the mayor was good and ready.

* * *

Pleasance would be so surprised.

Madame Pompeii had meant to take her to lunch for several days now, but other things always seemed to get in the way. She turned on the right blinker of Perry's Lexus sedan, knowing the intersection she needed was coming up in the next block or two. She hadn't even tried to use the GPS installed in the dash – the opinionated voice more of a nuisance than a help. She glanced in the rearview mirror and noticed a car crowding behind her, but she felt no pressure to speed up. If only everyone would take the time to appreciate this lovely summer day. Flowerboxes along the street bloomed with an explosion of color; children laughed and played in yards; neighbors stopped on sidewalks to chat, their leashed chickens pecking at the ground. Well, she could have done without that last image – a reminder of her failure to dispel the curse afflicting the town.

The car behind her began to honk its horn repeatedly, and she rolled down her window to motion it around her. Two teenagers in a sporty convertible squealed past the Lexus, one of them yelling at her, "Get a horse!"

She continued unhurried to Pleasance's place of employment. Maybe the Pork Barrel for lunch today. They always served a sumptuous buffet at noontime, enough to satisfy her niece's linebacker appetite. And the luncheon would provide the perfect opportunity to broach the subject of Pleasance's gentleman caller and her three Latin admirers. They obviously all cherished her, and yet she was rude to young Cappelli and had later run from the others at the Farmer's Market. There was such a thing as too much diffidence in matters of the heart. If Pleasance wasn't careful, she might lose their ardent attention altogether.

Perhaps better not to mention the appearance in town of the figure from her dream, the man with the gold lip ring. She couldn't put her finger on it, but something about the man disturbed her. And his interest in Pleasance at the film shoot did little to dissuade Madame Pompeii that his attentions might be less than honorable. The word "sinister" even came to mind as she thought about the way his eyes narrowed when he asked if anyone in the crowd knew who she was. Madame Pompeii shuddered as she approached the correct intersection and turned Perry's sedan onto the street that led to Pleasance's phone job.

When she pulled the car into the parking lot, she nearly pressed down the accelerator instead of the break when she saw that very same lip-ring man walking out the door of Telemarketing Enterprises. Not daring to look his way, she sat in the car until he got into his own vehicle and left.

She stepped out of the Lexus and went into the building, where a middle-aged man greeted her at the counter.

"Are you here for the job opening?" he asked.

Still flushed and breathless from her close encounter outside, she said, "What? Oh my, no."

"That's too bad. The two Todd losers just quit. Finally got a hundred dollar royalty check and walked out on me. They'll be back, but I need somebody now, pronto, right this minute!"

"Please, may I talk to Pleasance right away?"

The man dropped back into his swivel chair. "Popular person today. There was another guy just here looking for her."

"Where is she?"

"Who did you say you were?"

"I'm Madame – I mean, I'm her Aunt Penny. I was planning to take her out for lunch."

"She called earlier and said she wasn't coming in until this afternoon."

A chicken walked across the counter and the man got up and snuggled it under his arm.

"Well, can you tell me anything about that man who was looking for her?"

He shrugged, and with his free hand reached for a business card on his desk. "No, but he left her this."

Madame Pompeii leaned over the counter and plucked it from his hand. "I'll see that she gets it."

The man started to stutter, "I-I think I should give that to her."

But she was already walking out the door.

"Hey!" he called after her. "You sure you don't want a job?"

* * *

Proust no longer enjoyed his nighttime walk. After the seventeenth turn around the City Hall block, he'd quit pulling against the leash, and he'd long since marked everything that was markable. Lela was also tired of pretending that she and her dog were merely out for a stroll.

She looked up at the north window on the second floor, still unshaded. How could Earl Bob ignore the instructions? How could he ignore Bob and Arno?

One more pass, that's what she'd give it, and dragged Proust toward the corner. Her cell phone rang, and she flipped it open.

"Hello?"

"Is this 001?"

"Of course it is!" she barked into the mouthpiece. "Who else would answer this phone?"

"Oh, yeah, well, right. Any sign of a signal yet?"

Lela looked up at the window once more, hoping that in the past fifteen seconds, Earl Bob had moved the shade.

"Negative. What's your position?"

"We're already at the campground. We locked Bob and Arno in the outhouse. Pretty snug; it's a one-holer."

"Did you hide the cars?"

"Yep."

The note Howard delivered had instructed Earl Bob to leave the chicken-loving detainees at the entrance and drive eight hundred feet further to the other end of the campground. There he'd find a note telling him where to locate Bob and Arno. In the meantime, the resistance group, who would be hiding in the trees, would collect the detainees and make a dash through the forest for their cars.

"Uh, Lela – I mean, 001 – did you tell Earl Bob not to bring the cops?"

Proust started whining, and she jerked the leash to shut him up. Oh dear, the cops. It hadn't even occurred to her to mention that detail in the note. "I probably did."

"Probably?"

"Let's just worry about the plan."

"You coming out here pretty soon then?"

"I think I will." All the circles she'd walked around City Hall had begun to give her shin splints, and Proust didn't look like he could make another pass. "Maybe Earl Bob just forgot to signal us and is planning to go out there tonight yet. I'll see you in a few minutes."

She closed her phone and dragged the pug to the car. She struggled to lift him into the back seat, got in herself, and drove the five miles to the campground.

If Earl Bob didn't come through, she didn't know how they could continue to hold their prisoners. Bob had refused to talk to them anymore and turned his back every time they'd given him his TV dinner. Arno had turned religious, calling out for God to smite his enemies for their transgressions and to save him from persecution. He'd adopted the parlance of Charleton Heston in *The Ten Commandments*.

"Oh ye sinners," he would sometimes shout. "Let my people go!"

Of course, he just meant him and Bob, Lela supposed.

She drove past the campground and pulled her car off the road where she knew she'd find the Gremlin. She killed the lights and turned around to Proust. "Stay, boy." The dog didn't even lift his head off the seat. With a little flashlight as a guide, she walked through the trees until she came to the campground clearing. There, six of her comrades sat around a blazing fire ring, threading something onto sticks.

"Is this a hostage situation or a Campfire Girl outing?" Lela asked.

Denton looked up at her. "We didn't know when Earl Bob was going to get here. Helen had marshmallows."

In the distance, Lela could hear from the outhouse evangelistic admonishments from Arno. Both men pounded on the door.

Denton handed her a stick. "Might as well join us."

Half an hour later, the fire had reduced to glowing embers, but Lela could still make out the glum faces around her. Bob and Arno had stopped protesting and a depressing silence settled over the group. It looked like the prisoner exchange might be a bust.

But just as Lela was about to suggest they pack up their captives and head back to the detention barn, Duke jumped up and pointed at the road. "Look! Someone's coming."

Everyone else rose to their feet and strained to see. A single, dim light skimmed along the center of the highway about two feet off the ground, seeming to wobble and dodge the potholes in the road.

"What is that?" Helen asked.

"It's a bicycle," Denton said. The light was turning into the campground. "Quick! Back into the trees!"

Without making any sounds, the group watched the bicycle's approach. The rider stopped by the fire ring and got off. In the dim light of the glowing ashes, Lela recognized Howard.

He looked around and in a timid voice, called out, "Hello? I have a note for you aliens. It's from Mr. Jackson." He stood there a moment longer and then placed a piece of paper under a nearby rock. "Okay, then. I set the note right here."

He got back on his bike and began to pedal out of the campground and toward town. When he was out of sight, Duke dashed over to the rock and retrieved the note. He ran back to the others. They gathered around him while Denton switched on a flashlight.

"No deal," Denton read aloud.

Lela grabbed the note and read it herself. Just two words. Earl Bob wasn't going to make any exchange. He'd called their bluff.

They all groaned in disappointment and headed back to the fire ring.

"What do we do now?" Helen asked, dropping down on a rock.

Everyone looked from one to the other. Denton scratched his head; Felicia threw up her hands.

"Well, it's clear what we have to do," Duke said. "We have to eliminate Bob and Arno."

"Duke! What are you saying?" Felicia demanded. "We'll do no such thing."

"Of course, we won't eliminate them," Lela said. "We'll have to think of something else."

Denton picked up a marshmallow stick and stirred the embers. "We should let them go."

"What?" Helen asked. "How will we get our chicken friends released?"

"I think that's a moot point right now." Denton stood and started to walk toward the outhouse.

"Wait!" Lela called out. She walked over to him with a paper sack. "Wear this."

CHAPTER ELEVEN

Pleasance brushed sagebrush leaves from her pants and walked into Telemarketing Enterprises. After seeing The Three Fools at the excavation site, she'd made a decision about her immediate future. Phone sex wouldn't be part of it. But she thought it only fair to tell Pat about her resignation face to face. With any luck, she'd have those artifacts in her hands by early tomorrow morning and be on a plane to New York by noon.

"Thank God you're here!" Pat said. He came around the counter and virtually met her at the door. "The Todds walked out. No notice or anything." Lights flashed in every cubicle, and his eyes darted from phone to phone.

"Well, I need to talk to you about that."

"Talk to me about what?" Now he really seemed scared.

"I'm quitting, too."

"You can't do this to me! There's no one here to help."

Pleasance felt a little guilty about Pat's dilemma, but her time in Silverville was short now. In some ways, she regretted leaving a job she'd learned to enjoy. Becoming Honeysuckle-the-Dominatrix had been liberating, not to mention a power trip. She'd seldom worked a job where she *and* her clients received such immediate gratification. "I'm sorry, Pat. Change of plans and I just can't stay."

"Oh, crap. Look at that row of flashing caller buttons. Can you at least finish your shift this afternoon?"

"Not really. I've got some things to get ready before tonight."

"Oh come on, just a few more hours. Until I can get someone else in here." He gave her his best pathetic puppy-dog look. "Please?"

She sighed. Hoping to get to the house before Perry returned from the golf course, Pleasance intended to help herself to some specific items in the garage. And she didn't want to explain. If she waited until after dinner, she'd have to think of a way to preoccupy her uncle while she borrowed his gear. Of course, the later she delayed starting, the less likely she'd run into any interference. Grady and his treasure-hunting buddies would be sound asleep when she drove out to the site.

"Pat, you'll have to make this worth my time."

He hesitated for a moment, but she figured all those blinking phone lights couldn't stall him for long.

Then he said, "I'll pay you double-time."

"Double-time and a half."

"Okay. It's a deal."

"But I'm not staying past five."

"Thank you!" He pushed her toward her cubicle, and she sat down.

Pulling on her headset, she punched the first flashing button.

* * *

Three and a half hours later, Pleasance drove into Perry and Lela's driveway. Aunt Penny stood in the door and waited for her to get out of the car.

"Thank God you're here. We need to talk." Her aunt almost pushed her through the entrance and into the living room.

"What's wrong?"

"He's here in town, looking for you."

Pleasance flopped into a recliner. "Slow down, Aunt Penny. What are you talking about?"

"Do you remember me telling you about my dream of a man with a lip ring?"

"Sort of. Why?"

"I saw him downtown at that film shoot asking about you. I saw him again walking out of Telemarketing Enterprises."

"You came to my workplace?"

"Listen to me." Madame Pompeii rummaged in her purse until she produced a business card. "He left this for you."

Pleasance took the card. In plain lettering, it read, "Creative Solutions." Underneath was a phone number. She looked at her aunt. "So?"

"This man is dangerous, Pleasance. I can tell by his aura. Maybe you should get out of town."

Pandora began to squawk from her cage. "Action! Action! New scene!"

"Shut up, Pandora." Madame Pompeii stomped her foot at the parrot. "See, even this stupid bird thinks you need a change of scenery."

Pleasance laughed and she looked again at the card. The number's prefix was the same as Winchester's. The laugh died in her throat.

"Would you excuse me a minute?" she asked her aunt.

She stepped into the bedroom carrying the card. "Creative Solutions" – the very name said nothing, but it implied a whole range of problem-solving. Was she the problem? Possibly for Winchester. What if he'd sent somebody to settle accounts? Or to make an example of her. She hadn't come up with the treasure yet, and it'd been well over a week now – the week he'd given her to honor her part of the bargain. Her first inclination was to call and explain, but would that just bring her back up on his radar? She hoped the nose-ring man had no connection.

She pulled off her boots and padded into the kitchen to make a peanut butter sandwich. Opening the refrigerator door, she stared at the shelves, wondering what she was looking for. Nothing in the fridge. *Get hold of yourself, Pleasance. Concentrate.* She closed the door and went to the pantry to pull out the peanut butter. She unscrewed the lid, set the jar on the counter, and pulled a knife from the drawer. She walked back into the bedroom, just knife in hand.

When she sat back down on the bed, she looked at the utensil. What was she doing with just a knife? She would have found her distraction amusing if her life might not have hung in the balance.

To hell with it. She pulled out her cell phone, knowing the number by heart.

Two rings and she heard a voice. "Mr. Winchester's office."

"This is Pleasance Pantiwycke. I need to talk to your boss."

The secretary asked her to hold.

She couldn't get Cap out of her head, and how he'd had to disappear when he fell short of Winchester's expectations. If he hadn't made himself scarce, would he have met a lip-ring man in a dark alley?

She noticed her hand shaking a little when the secretary's voice returned to the phone. "I'm sorry, Miss Pantiwycke. He doesn't want to talk to you."

Pleasance tasted bile in the back of her throat. "I need to speak with him now. It's important."

The polite voice on the other end of the line replied, "I'm afraid that's not possible. Have a good day." The secretary hung up, leaving Pleasance holding a dead phone.

Oh God, why couldn't he have waited just one more day? She'd likely have those artifacts in hand in less than twelve hours. She considered her options. Maybe she *should* skip town like Cap did. But Cap had connections she didn't have. Winchester would find her eventually. Pleasance needed to buy herself some time. Needed to prove to the billionaire that she could deliver the goods. But right now, she had to deal with this lip-ring guy before he had an opportunity to deal with her.

She strode back through the living room toward the front door. "Thanks, Aunt Penny, for the heads-up."

"Where are you going?"

"Out."

Pleasance left the house, got in her car, and backed out the driveway. She took one more glance at the business card and steered the vehicle toward the Last Call Cowboy Bar.

* * *

Lela studied Carl, who sat across the table from her and Perry. He calmly sipped a cup of coffee.

"Bob said the ringleader had long narrow feet," Carl said.

Lela curled her toes – even though the table hid them from the sheriff's view. She'd always hated her feet, but she didn't think other people had ever noticed their length. Long, narrow, and flat, which maybe made her a good swimmer, but right now they felt like conspicuous flippers attached to the bottoms of her ankles.

"What are you saying, Carl?" Perry started to raise his voice. "Are you accusing Lela of kidnapping Bob and Arno?"

"I'm sorry, but she's a person of interest in this investigation. And, after all, she does have a history of getting involved in conspiracies in this town."

Lela winced. He referred, of course, to the incident two years ago when she masterminded the plan to rid the town of tourists during all the UFO hysteria. But she wasn't the only one in that little group. "If you recall, other people participated in that fiasco, including you, Bob, and even Earl Bob."

Carl nodded. "I know. But you were the instigator in that plan, too. Which is why we thought of you. Let's have a look at your feet, Lela."

With reluctance, she swiveled in the chair to thrust out her feet. If only she hadn't worn those green stockings with red chickens today.

"Nice socks." Carl grinned as he inspected her footwear.

Perry jumped up from the table. "Balderdash! Lela had nothing to do with this. There are lots of people with long feet. Look at your own."

"But Arno said the leader was short and, excuse me, Lela, um, stout. That narrows the field quite a bit."

Lela scooted her red chickens back under the table.

Carl continued, "You know kidnapping is a federal offense. By all rights, I should be involving the FBI, but Earl Bob wants us to work this out among ourselves."

Lela heard a loud thump coming from one of the bedrooms, followed by Madame Pompeii rolling into the hallway. The woman stood up, straightened her muumuu, and tried to look dignified. That bedroom door latch never did work very well. It wouldn't have taken much for Madame Pompeii to lean against and knock it open. Obviously, she'd been trying to eavesdrop.

"Pardon me," the psychic said, strutting into the kitchen. "I couldn't help but overhear. Lela could have nothing to do with these preposterous charges."

Carl asked, "You can vouch for her during this whole time?"

"Don't be ridiculous. I'm a clairvoyant, not a watchdog. But if she were involved in this crime, I'd have sensed it. Her aura would have betrayed her. And I see nothing remotely suggestive in her spiritual emanations. You clearly have the wrong person."

"Uh-huh," Carl said, and turned back to face Lela.

Perry paced back and forth in front of the sink. "It'll take more than long feet and short stature to accuse Lela of –"

"Hold on, Perry. I'm not accusing anybody of anything. Not yet, anyway. I just said Lela was a person of interest."

"Well, you can't prove anything."

"That's right, I can't. I was just hoping Lela would come forward if she had any information."

Lela figured that was her cue to confess. However, if she did, Carl would pressure her to name the co-conspirators. Since she had talked them into the kidnapping scheme to begin with, she felt a certain loyalty to protect them.

Better not to admit anything.

An uncomfortable silence filled the kitchen. Finally, Lela said, "I can't help you."

Perry stopped pacing and rejoined his wife and the sheriff at the table. "Doesn't sound like Bob and Arno are any worse for the wear."

"Well, they might argue differently," Carl said. "According to Arno, they suffered subhuman conditions. Their captors kept them in a chicken coop for two nights and only fed them frozen tamale TV dinners."

"But they weren't tortured or anything," Perry persisted.

"Not unless you count the bar of soap the kidnappers crammed into Arno's mouth."

Uninvited, Madame Pompeii sat down. "Some police departments hire psychics to help them solve crimes."

"Uh-huh," Carl said again. "Lela, do you have any idea who might be behind this?"

"Like I said, I can't help you."

"Can't or won't?"

Lela said nothing, which gave Madame Pompeii an opportunity to break in. "In fact, some police departments *welcome* psychics on their more difficult cases. It seems to me that –"

"I think you're way out of line here, sheriff." Perry was clearly getting agitated again. "This is bordering on harassment."

"Perry, Carl is only doing his job," Lela said.

"I think it's time for the sheriff to leave."

Carl stood. "I'm sorry to have disturbed you folks. Lela, if you think of anything – anything at all – you know how to get in touch." He put on his hat, tipped it to both women, and headed for the front door.

Perry waited until they all heard the screen door bang shut. He turned to Lela. "You're involved in this, aren't you." It wasn't a question.

"Of course, she's not! Hasn't anyone been listening to me?" Madame Pompeii appeared disgusted. "I told you before, I would know if she were guilty."

A look passed between Lela and Perry.

Proust trotted into the kitchen and sat down next to his empty bowl. His feline nemesis, Ptolemy, sauntered in after him and jumped on the counter, an expectant dinnertime look in his eyes.

"Well, I guess we ought to think about eating," Perry suggested.

Lela got up and went to the refrigerator. "Yes, Perry, I think that's a good idea."

"What are we having?"

She opened the freezer. "Tamale TV dinners okay?"

* * *

Pleasance glanced around The Last Call Cowboy Bar. Too early for much of a crowd to choose from, but she'd have to make do. She sat on a bar stool and ordered a Coors Light. The jukebox in the corner blared honky-tonk. No cigarette haze, but several spittoons stood at strategic points throughout the room. In the lowered light, she could just make out a collection of ranch brands burned into the wood paneling on one wall.

Four cowboys clustered around a pool table, a line of empty beer bottles sitting on a nearby bench. From the looks of those guys, they must have been used to setting miles of fence posts and bucking bales of hay. The biggest of the group – standing six-foot-four and all lean, hard muscle – aimed his hat at a moose head mounted on the wall and gave it a toss. The others whooped when it landed squarely on the antler.

151

Pleasance applauded the feat – loud enough for the young cowboys to hear. All eyes around the pool table turned her way, and the big one walked over. He staggered just a little. "Evening, darlin'. Can I buy you a drink?" With his Stetson on the antlers, there was nothing to hide the plastered hair that ringed his head from a tight-fitting brim.

She let her chin quiver and turned back to her beer. "I think I'd better drink alone."

He slid onto the next stool and dropped an arm around her shoulder. "Now that ain't no way to be sociable. C'mon over and have a drink with me and the boys."

She protested just enough to make him more insistent. He took her hand and guided her over to the table under the moose.

"You just set yourself down, and I'll go get you that drink." He waved his pool-playing buddies over and moseyed to the bar. The others put their cue sticks down and came over.

Looking demure as she could, Pleasance lowered her eyelashes and offered a shy grin. "This is real nice of you guys." She burst into tears.

About that time, the big cowboy returned with a new beer. "Whoa! What's wrong? Bubba doesn't let any little lady cry like that."

And she told them her story. The longer she talked, the more riled they became – and she excused herself to the ladies' room.

Once inside, she dug out the business card and called the number.

"This is Antoine."

"Creative Solutions?"

"You got it."

She leaned against the wall and took a deep breath. "This is Pleasance Pantiwycke. I know who you work for and why you're looking for me."

He laughed. "Well then, that makes my job a little easier."

Holy shit! What a flippant attitude for someone hired to eliminate her. Swallowing hard, she continued, "Let's meet in a public place and discuss this."

"You name it and I'll be there."

He sounded too damn eager.

"Okay, at The Last Call Cowboy Bar on Frontage Road. Now."

"Works for me." And he hung up.

Pleasance went back to her new friends and sat down. A fresh beer waited for her.

For the next thirty minutes, she learned that all four men worked for a rancher named Merle. One of the guys broke his wrist during branding last year, another went to junior college on a rodeo scholarship, and a third was partial to mules.

"Better than a horse in the high-country," he claimed.

Bubba shook his head. "Ain't never had a mule. Ain't never gonna. They're mean." He showed Pleasance the scar on his forearm where his friend's mount had bitten him two summers before.

The mule owner burst out laughing. "Bubba, you gotta learn to work with them. They don't work with you."

What surprised Pleasance the most was how polite they all were. Treated her like a real lady. No groping and no swearing.

A new singer's voice rolled out of the jukebox, and Bubba jumped from his chair. "This is my song!"

He took Pleasance by the elbow and led her to the small dance floor. Bubba two-stepped like a pro, grinning and singing the song word for word. She didn't know the steps, but she tried to stay with him. Holding his hand in one of hers, she kept a beer in the other, occasionally taking a swig. When Bubba twirled her around, some of the beer sloshed onto the floor, and he slipped, almost falling. The acrobatics sent everybody into a fit of laughter. This was a side of Silverville she'd never seen before. She liked it.

The song ended and they headed back to the table. At that point, a cowbell over the door jingled and in walked the lip-ring man.

"That's him," she whispered across the table.

All four cowboys got up as she leaned back to finish her beer.

* * *

A chair sailed past her ear.

Every now and then, the lip-ring man's head tried to crawl out of the cowboy pile on top of him.

Maybe she had laid it on a little thick earlier.

"I can't believe he left me," she'd told the cowboys. "And for a man."

It really seemed to light a fire under them. Bubba slapped his hand on the table. "That just ain't right!"

"The lip ring should have tipped me off," Pleasance said, dabbing a napkin to her eyes.

The damsel-in-distress act had set those cowboys hell bent on saving her honor. At least, that's how it appeared, judging from that pile of arms and boots scuffling on the floor in front of the bar.

Pulling himself out of the fight, Bubba staggered over to her. His eye was swollen shut. "I think we've just about got him talked outta being gay."

"Thanks, Bubba. But don't kill him."

"No, ma'am." He winked at her through his good eye and dived back into the brawl.

No, she wouldn't let them do to him what he probably had planned for her. She just needed to slow this Antoine down until she nabbed the artifacts and delivered them to Winchester.

She stood, blew Bubba a kiss, and left the bar.

* * *

When Pleasance got back to the house, the only light on was in the garage. Through the window, she could see the top of Uncle Perry's head leaning over a bench. Damn, she needed him out of there so she could collect the equipment.

She poked her head inside. "What are you doing? You're usually in bed at this hour."

"I wish I was." He had stacked a small collection of tools on the bench. "But we had a little excitement at the house earlier this evening."

He told her about Carl's visit.

"And you're pretty sure Aunt Lela was a part of it?"

"No question." He pointed to the tools. "First thing in the morning, that partially built chicken coop is coming down."

"She's not gonna like it."

"She doesn't have a choice. I've made an executive decision."

Pleasance nodded and glanced over at the box she wanted to plunder for the night. "Let me help you get that stuff into the back yard, so you can get to bed." She grabbed the pick and shovel and followed him out the garage door.

Halfway across the yard, he spun around. "Oops, forgot the light."

"I'll get it," she said, and shepherded him toward the house. She dropped the tools by the back door, and they both stepped through the utility room and into the kitchen.

Perry flipped on the hall light. "Well, I'll say good night."

"Before you turn in, I should mention that I won't be in Silverville much longer."

"Oh?"

"There may be an acquisition project coming up."

"Then I suppose you'll be off on another adventure." He spoke with almost a tinge of envy. "Where is it this time? Thailand? Peru?"

"Something like that." She felt a stab of guilt for not coming clean about what she really planned to do. She'd always been closer to her uncle than her own father. But what initially began as a trip to stall Winchester had snowballed into a bona fide treasure hunt. A hunt with potentially dangerous opponents that she preferred to tackle without Perry. This would've been an easier job with Cap's help. Maybe she should've told him after all.

"Gosh, I wish I could go with you." His face lit up. "Diving for sunken gold, spelunking for ancient scrolls, escaping Bedouins – best times of my life."

"Not this time, Uncle Perry."

"Yeah, you're right. I can't afford to be that far away. God knows what your Aunt Lela will do next."

"Go to bed. I'm going to turn off that garage light."

He grinned. "Knock 'em dead, Kiddo – well, figuratively." And he walked down the hall.

Pleasance returned to the garage to pull down the boxes that contained the gear she thought she'd need. Ropes, carabiners, diving mask, oxygen tank. She laid everything on the floor and made a mental checklist. The tank needed filling, and she had yet to find a wet suit for cold-water diving.

As she worked, the half-truths she'd told Uncle Perry still nagged at her. They'd always been a good team. And, of course, his best times *were* treasure-hunting. These days his life pretty much consisted of playing an occasional round of golf – and keeping tabs on a wife with a chicken fetish.

Crouching over the equipment, Pleasance heard the garage door open and Perry come in. For a few moments, he said nothing, just surveyed the items strewn on the floor.

"Uh, I thought if you didn't mind," she stammered. "I'd borrow some of these –"

"The air compressor is behind the freezer."

His calm acceptance of her clandestine behavior overwhelmed her. She felt a spasm of guilt that threatened to derail her secrecy. "I haven't exactly been straight with you."

Perry looked at his wristwatch and squatted beside her. "Okay. I've got all night."

"Won't take that long." In the span of ten minutes, she'd confessed almost everything – her plan for the artifacts, the arrival of The Three Fools, Winchester's threat. She didn't mention Cap.

When she finished, Perry turned his head away from her, his shoulders trembling. Oh, God, she hadn't expected his reaction to be so severe. Was it the fact that she'd hidden her true occupation from him, or that she'd come to Silverville with ulterior motives? Either way, she must have totally disappointed him.

Pleasance jumped up and stepped in front of him. "Uncle Perry, I'm so sorry."

But when he lifted his head, he was laughing so hard he fell off his haunches and onto his backside. "My God, girl, did you think I believed that stupid story of you working for a museum?"

She ran her tongue over dry lips. "Yeah, I guess I did."

"Lela might, but not me. Not for a minute." He raised a hand. "Here, pull me up."

Pleasance yanked him to his feet.

He picked up the rope and started to recoil it. "Hot damn! What time are we leaving for the cave?"

* * *

The headlights of the Land Rover pointed at the cave while they unloaded their gear. Pleasance hoisted the oxygen tank over her shoulder and Perry gathered rope and wetsuit. Both already wore headlamps to guide them over the rocks toward the dark cavern's mouth.

"Don't forget the bags," Pleasance reminded her uncle. They'd rummaged through the garage until they found two large canvas duffels to collect anything they might find.

"Hopeful, aren't you?"

"I've already seen Grady throw an artifact back inside." She picked her way up the slope.

Pleasance lowered her forehead to focus the headlamp beam on the rubble. As she stepped into the cave, she called behind her, "Be careful when you get up here. It's wet and slippery."

Lifting a leg over several basketball-sized boulders, she ducked through the opening and panned the light across the interior, which looked to be about four yards wide and dozen or so deep. At her feet, a narrow stream of water still flowed out of the cave. She followed the trickle to a deeper pool a little further inside. Guessing there was more volume than she could see, Pleasance decided this must be the aquifer that Grady had told her uncle about. Bubbles periodically broke on the surface at the far end – probably a pocket of air coming from the deeper recesses of the aquifer.

A glistening trinket, deposited on the bank to the right, caught her eye. She moved over to get a better look. A buckle. Perhaps the same object Grady had tossed back into the cave. Higher up the sloping floor, several coins twinkled from the light of her headlamp beam.

"See anything?" Perry asked, scrambling though the mouth.

If only she could have reported what archaeologist Howard Carter first said when he looked into King Tut's tomb: *Yes, wonderful things!* But so far, she didn't see much.

Perry panted up beside her and dropped the gear. Their separate beams played over the ground and walls, assessing the site. She saw his light pause on the buckle and nearby coins.

"Are you thinking what I'm thinking?" Pleasance asked.

"That the water washed these things up?"

"Uh-huh." She motioned toward the pool. "The artifacts are down there now."

He handed her the wetsuit. "I'll turn around."

Pleasance pulled off her clothes and struggled to tug on the neoprene second skin. Resting her butt against a rock, she tried to maneuver the suit legs over her calves. There was no way she could wrestle them up unless she stood. Inching and stretching the material higher up her thighs with loud snaps, she jumped and shimmied into it.

"Doin' okay over there?" Uncle Perry asked.

"Yeah. Just more trouble to put this thing on than I remembered."

Once she got the suit to her waist, she reached behind to slide in her arms. The biggest chore proved closing the zipper over her breasts. She exhaled and caved her shoulders just to get the zipper to the level of a low-cut evening dress.

"Who's wetsuit is this, Uncle Perry?"

"It's yours. I bought it for you when you were fourteen."

She stretched over to pick up the goggles, but the suit didn't have enough give. It felt like a toe-touch exercise inside a giant rubber band. "I could use a little help over here."

Perry turned toward her. He shined his light the length and breadth of her body. "Can you swim like that?"

"If you help me put on my flippers, I can."

Once fully equipped, Pleasance duck-walked over to the bank, her knees stiff and unyielding. Perry helped lower her into the water. Before she fitted the oxygen regulator into her mouth, she looked at her uncle. "I'm sure glad you came along."

"*Viel Spaß!*"

Well, maybe it wouldn't be fun, but hopefully lucrative.

Adjusting her regulator and goggles, she dropped below the surface. She played the headlamp through the murky water and edged down the cave wall, letting her fingers push against the rock to guide her movement. She reached the floor of the cavity a mere eight feet down, and she tried to fold her knees to touch bottom. Sediment swirled at every swipe she made, her fingers ghostly in the short span of the beam. Almost blindly, she groped the immediate vicinity until her hand swept over something small and round. She plucked it from the mud and held it close to her face. A ring set with a large ruby. A single small carpal bone still poked through the center. She pulled out the bone and let it drop.

Clutching her prize, Pleasance pushed off the aquifer floor and bounded to the surface, where Perry stood overlooking the pool. She waved the ring in the air and removed her regulator. "There's stuff down here, but it's hard to see."

Perry took the ring. He grinned. "Sort of like old times."

Pleasance repositioned her goggles to give them a tighter fit around her face and dropped back down into the water. No time to dally. This would be her only chance to nab anything that might be in the pool. Then she wondered just how big that pool would turn out to be. In her experience, a lot of these underground rivers extended back for hundreds of feet, winding and twisting like random mazes. She returned to the surface.

"Uncle Perry, toss me one end of the rope."

"Need a life line?"

She nodded. When he pitched her several coils, she looped one end around her waist, securing it with a double bowline knot. She plunged back into the pool.

The ring already made the trip worthwhile, and the stone alone might amount to more than what she owed Winchester. A few more artifacts and she'd be able to rent an apartment in the upper west end of New York. She might buy herself a paraplane. Hell, she'd buy two and give one to Uncle Perry. She kicked her flippers and cruised close to the floor until she came to the rock wall at the far end of the cave. Hand over hand, Pleasance followed along the side and discovered another opening that turned sharply to the right. It was tight, but she squeezed through into a separate chamber. Her foot brushed against something solid. It teetered, stirring up more sediment. When she circled around to investigate, the object simply looked like a smooth, rounded rock. But it moved too easily, looked too symmetrical. Scooping the half-sphere from the mud, she turned it over and brought it closer to her goggles for a better look.

A Conquistador helmet, and in one piece.

In a frenzy, she jammed her hands into the mud, swiping them back and forth for a feel of anything else. Clouds of residue filled her line of vision, and then the back of her hand disturbed another moveable object. The end of it dislodged and appeared from the sediment, exposing the length of a long, thin sword. Pleasance ran her fingers along the blade to find the hilt and worked it out of the mud. One hand held the helmet and the other the sword – all she could carry on this trip.

Back at the bank edge, she poked her head out of the water. "You know how to fly a paraplane?"

"Huh?"

Pleasance hoisted the two artifacts above the surface.

"Hot damn!" Perry took the helmet and sword. "These might be worth a few bucks."

"Heading back down."

Her uncle turned his headlamp to his wristwatch. "Better make it quick. Sun will be up in a couple of hours."

She dived down into the pool and started back toward the cavern chamber. But she hadn't quite reached the opening when she noticed a dull glimmer to her left. A medallion? Stretching sideways to retrieve an oval-shaped object, her knuckles brushed against something semi-soft, something organic and black attached to the medallion. She allowed her fingers to trail up a tube-like structure. She kicked to move closer.

To her surprise, she recognized the tube as an arm, fully articulated, attached to shoulder, neck, chin – and another pair of goggles. Through the visor, eyes stared back at her. One winked.

She tore the regulator from her mouth. "Maurice, you old bastard!" she gurgled, choking on cave water.

The last time she'd seen him was sprawled on a New York sidewalk, cursing and shouting in pain after she'd kicked his walker out from underneath him. But he'd overheard that she was heading to Silverville. He must have followed. She should have guessed he'd do something like this.

Bobbing to the top, Pleasance coughed and called to her uncle. "Get the artifacts out of here! Quick!"

"We will be happy to do that, señorita."

At the familiar voice, Pleasance tore off the goggles with one hand while treading water with the other. She squinted at the bank, where she'd left her uncle. Three figures shadowed him, not quite visible from the beam of her headlamp. One of them trained a flashlight on her.

"Come out of the water, por favor," Mocoso said. "And bring anything else you have found. It would be best for your partner."

Mocoso and Rizoso held her uncle between them. It looked like they'd tied Perry's hands behind his back.

* * *

In wary strokes Pleasance swam toward the bank, her brain numb with confusion. She looked behind her and there was no sign of Maurice. Was he in collusion with The Three Fools? He had stolen from them, too, but of course, they didn't know that. They had blamed her for absconding with the jade mask.

When she arrived at the bank, Lorenzo thrust out a hand to pull her out. Pleasance grasped it, said *gracias,* and used all the strength in her shoulders to yank him over her head and into the water. He screamed and landed in a noisy back flop. Still gripping his wrist, she pulled Lorenzo to her, placing both her hands on the top of his head and pushing downwards as hard as she could.

Lorenzo's arms thrashed and churned as he tried to emerge. Pleasance let him up once to gulp air and then shoved him down again, holding him under.

"Let my uncle go, or I'll drown your friend."

"Go ahead. He's a bumbling *idiota,*" Mocoso answered. The glint of a revolver pointed at Perry's temple. "That will not help your uncle."

She relaxed her hold on the struggling fool. He fought his way to the surface, choking and gasping for air.

"I'm coming out. Just don't hurt him."

They both climbed out of the pool. Pleasance waddled over to Perry as fast as her wetsuit and flippers would let her. "You okay?"

"Sorry. They got the jump on me."

Mocoso wagged the gun. "No more talking!" He picked up the duffel and forced it into her hands. "Put the treasure in the bag. All of it!"

She opened the duffel and tried to stoop to pick up the helmet, but the wetsuit was too tight. "I can't. You'll have to untie my uncle so he can help me."

All three thieves exchanged glances. After a moment of hesitation, Mocoso said, "This is a trick."

Pleasance spread her arms, pretending that the suit restricted her more than it did. "No it's not. Look at me."

They did. Right at her cleavage.

Mocoso motioned to Rizoso. "Untie the man." He cocked the weapon. "But remember. I have the gun."

While Uncle Perry collected the helmet and other artifacts and began to drop them into the bag, Pleasance glanced over at the pool. Where was Maurice? Why hadn't he shown up during all this? If he was working with The Three Fools, there was no reason to remain submerged. Or maybe he'd escaped through another opening in the cave once he saw trouble.

Perry gathered the last of the coins on the floor and pitched them into the duffel. "That's it. That's all of it." He handed the bag over to Rizoso.

Rizoso peered inside. "Only this?" He carried the artifacts over to Mocoso, who also looked in the duffel.

"Perhaps not yet," Mocoso said. "Once the *señorita* has returned our jade mask, we will have plenty."

Pleasance swung around to face him. "But I don't have – "

"Jade mask? I have it," a voice wafted across the pool.

They all turned to look into the water, aiming their flashlights where Maurice's head floated.

Mocoso, startled, fired three quick shots at Maurice, who disappeared into the aquifer. One of the shots missed the water and hit the far wall, ricocheting several times from rock to rock. Instinctively, most of them dropped to their knees to avoid the errant bullet. Mocoso and Rizoso rolled to the ground, holding their ears from the reverberating report of the gun. Lorenzo hot-footed in place, trying to dodge the missile zinging around the cavern.

It was all the opportunity Pleasance needed. She exchanged glances with Perry and they both made a dash for the cave mouth. Her uncle took the lead, scrambling over the boulders at the entrance. No way could she keep up with him, the wetsuit binding her like a full-body girdle and the flippers slapping ground like the feet of a lame penguin. And no way to maneuver around the dancing Lorenzo. She flattened him with a linebacker's rush. As she dived through the opening to clear the rocks, Pleasance plummeted down the slope, nearly colliding with Perry. He paused long enough to yank off her flippers and pull her upright, and then the two skidded nearly to the bottom of the narrow arroyo.

Behind them, the gun fired again, and Pleasance heard the snap of a bullet close to her ear.

"Stop, or I shoot you!"

She'd never outrun them with that wetsuit, and she came to a halt. Perry might have gotten away, but he stopped when she did.

"You can make it to the Rover. Keep going!" she hissed.

Perry shook his head and climbed the several feet back up to her. "I'm not leaving without you." He grinned. "Besides, I have a plan."

By this time, The Three Fools had descended the slope. Mocoso glared at Pleasance.

Lorenzo rubbed his arm and complained, "My elbow, it is broken."

Mocoso ignored him. "Very foolish, *señorita*. Now we have you and the treasure." He glanced around to his empty-handed companions. "Where is the bag?"

Lorenzo and Rizoso looked at each other. Rizoso pointed at his friend. "He forgot to bring it down!"

Lorenzo whined, "But my arm . . ."

"*Silencio!*" Mocoso barked. He motioned to Rizoso. "Go up and get it!"

The fool trudged back up to the cavern.

One hand holding the gun, Mocoso used the other to pull two short ropes out of his pocket. "Lorenzo, tie their wrists."

"But my arm!"

As they began to argue, Perry stepped closer to Pleasance and said in a loud voice, "Pleasance, why are you holding your head?"

"Huh?"

He urged her with a subtle gesture to raise her hands to her temples. "You look sick."

She stared at him, puzzled.

He whispered, "Remember Tunisia."

Of course! Tunisia, when they'd duped the Bedouins. Pleasance bent over and moaned. She fell to the ground and started to tremble.

"Oh my God, she's having a seizure!" Perry shouted.

Mocoso and Lorenzo stopped arguing and approached Pleasance.

She worked up a gob of spit and stirred with her tongue until it began to foam.

Perry wrung his hands. "Is she frothing at the mouth?"

The two captors leaned close to get a better look.

"I didn't think that mad dog had broken the skin when it bit her last week," Perry lied. "She's got rabies!"

Just as Mocoso and Lorenzo tried to scramble away, Pleasance rolled hard into their shins, pitching them forward. Perry used the momentum to grasp each by the back of the head and slam their faces down onto the rocks. Lorenzo slumped cold, but Mocoso staggered to his knees, a limp grip on the revolver. Pleasance tried to sit up before he had the chance to stand, but the wetsuit kept snapping her backwards.

"Oh shit," she muttered, and reached up with both hands, grabbed him by the ears, and slammed his nose against her forehead. He collapsed on the ground next to her, the gun clattering down the slope and out of sight.

Pleasance struggled to her feet just as Rizoso came tripping down the slope from the cave, dragging the duffel behind him.

"¡Dios mío!" he said, looking at his fallen friends.

"It's the curse," Perry said. "It may have killed them. And we're probably next."

Rizoso's eyes widened. Without checking the condition of the other two, he dropped the bag, turned, and ran the rest of the way down the hill to an old Chrysler. He jumped in and started the ignition, fishtailing away.

"That was easy." Pleasance picked up Mocoso's ropes from the ground. She tossed one to Perry, and they tied up the unconscious men.

"What do we do with these guys?" Perry asked, as he finished his knot.

"Leave them. They'll work themselves loose at some point."

"They'll come after us."

"Not after we sick the sheriff on them for being illegals." She picked up the duffel and looked down at her wetsuit. "I need my clothes, but under the circumstances, I think it would be faster for you to get them."

"But what about that other guy in the cave?"

Pleasance hoisted the duffel. "The treasure's not up there anymore. That means he's not either."

"Quite right, my dear," a disembodied voice said from behind a nearby boulder. Maurice stepped out. "I'm right beside you."

"Maurice, you old bastard!"

"Yes, it is I." His hair wasn't even mussed from the diving cap. "And you've forgotten something."

He held out his palm and let the medallion from the pool dangle by its chain. With laborious shuffles, the octogenarian approached her and motioned to open the bag. When she loosened the drawstrings, he outstretched a quaking hand and let the medallion drop inside.

"Who is this?" Perry asked.

"Find something to tie him up with." Pleasance reclosed the bag.

"But he's old!"

"Old and crafty. Don't trust him."

Perry hesitated.

"Hurry, Uncle Perry."

Perry yanked the belt from his pants and walked closer to the two. Maurice held out his hands, a willing captive waiting to be bound. But then he withdrew one hand and reached into his pocket.

"Oh, I have one more thing for you." Maurice thrust an object toward Perry, who tensed and doubled over onto the ground.

Pleasance had no time to react before Maurice turned to her. She felt the surge of an electrical charge, and the last thing she remembered was Maurice cradling her head as she crumpled.

CHAPTER TWELVE

The grays pushed the terrified man forward. Although the aliens stood no higher than his belt, he seemed powerless to resist their prodding.

"Please, no. Please!" He cowered as the strange creatures encircled him, forcing him to his knees before another waiting figure, who towered above them all.

"That is of no importance to us, Earthling." The giant alien reached forth large hands that ended in tentacle-like fingers, wrapping them around the man's head. The alien's bulbous, exposed brain pulsed with each word that it spoke. "Our minds will now meld, and you will become our minion."

The Earthling stiffened and fell forward. When he did, the tentacles remained fastened to the temples, leaving the head-honcho alien with a pair of gloveless human hands.

The spectators burst out laughing as the director stopped the shooting of the scene.

"Cheesy!" someone in the crowd shouted.

It was indeed, Madame Pompeii thought. Entertaining nevertheless, and certainly more exciting than the life she had led before coming to Silverville.

In her old hometown, nothing like this had ever happened. The Waterloo community followed the habitual rhythms of corn crops and John Deere's cycle of hirings and firings, almost never taking advantage of her paranormal gifts. She'd tried to bring a sense of magic to the town. One year, she organized a psychic fair, but no one came. And she couldn't find any psychics – aside from herself – anyway. She'd even planted a sign in her front yard, offering aura and past-life readings. It only lasted two weeks before police told her she was violating residential ordinances. At least her job as a nursing home activities director had given her the opportunity to enrich the lives of old people.

There, she'd frequently arranged for school children to present singing programs. Sometimes she found owners willing to bring pets. Even the more withdrawn residents responded to that. And each day, without fail, she held exercise classes. Never mind that those in wheelchairs could only extend their legs a few inches beyond their footrests.

But somehow she sensed they needed more.

The idea struck her that a séance could be quite stimulating. One evening after dinner, she collected her charges from across the facility and placed them around a large table normally used for crafts. Madame Pompeii assumed they would be ideal participants since the majority of their acquaintances had already passed over.

She had lowered the lights and set out an array of candles.

"Does anyone have a loved one you'd like to contact?" she'd asked the group.

"Weren't we getting ice-cream for dessert?" one timid voice asked.

"After the séance." Madame Pompeii scanned the participants. "Hannah, perhaps you would like to talk to your husband."

"Not in a million years." The old woman rolled her eyes. "Happiest day of my life was when the combine ran him over."

Madame Pompeii focused on the man sitting next to Hannah. "How about you, Herbert? Surely you'd like to communicate with your sister?"

Herbert pushed his wheelchair back from the table and rolled himself out of the room.

"Okay, let me try this." Madame Pompeii raised her hands and tilted her head upward. "Is there anyone from the other side who would like to speak to a loved one here? Show us a sign."

"Wait a minute," a resident gasped. "I hear something!"

What she heard was the head nurse storming into the activities room, Herbert wheeling his chair right behind.

"What's going on here?" the nurse demanded.

It was Madame Pompeii's last day at the nursing home. Right afterwards, she packed up and left for Silverville – with no particular plans for the future.

The shout of a man snapped her out of her reveries. "We need the extras at the other end of the street! The second unit director is setting up."

Madame Pompeii sauntered along with the other spectators to the new location, enjoying the chance to see the backstage movie-making process. Maybe she should move to Hollywood. She could get a job there at a nursing home, a nursing home filled with aging film stars and eccentric, interesting characters. They were probably quite familiar with séances.

"Oh, excuse me, Mrs. Poupon," she heard a voice say at the same time someone stepped on her foot. It was Howard.

"Quite alright. At least you chose the foot without corns." She smiled at him.

He smiled back and began to pick his ear. Two costumed actors brushed past them and he said, "Those are fake aliens. I know the real ones."

"Of course, you do."

"Well, I'm looking for Otto. Bye." He backed away, turned, and stepped on the toe of the very next person.

Now, *there* was an eccentric character. And Grady. And Kandy-B-Good. Even Pat Montgomery showed signs of eccentricity.

When she arrived at the second location, the crew was laying track to roll a camera alongside the scene. Men pulled strange-looking equipment from a van and began to attach it to scaffolding.

"Test it this time to make sure the fog comes out in the right direction," a woman barked.

It took Madame Pompeii just a moment to recognize the voice. Kandy – well, Candace now. Such a shame that she had thrown away her calling. Now that tent would be empty ... unless, unless another reputable psychic took her place. But, of course, that would just be a summer job. And Perry and Lela couldn't be expected to support her through the winters.

Tourist towns offered little in the way of employment except during high-traffic seasons. It would be harder to find something the rest of the year.

Wait a minute. Someone had offered her a job recently. Pat Montgomery. Maybe she'd been too quick to decline. She could be good on the phone and, certainly, she could sell whatever he was marketing. Perhaps she'd talk to him about the position.

Fog began to roll across the set, blanketing everything in an eerily translucent mist. Two actor-aliens stood in the center. On the far side, she could just make out a man throwing the switch on a large humming coil, and a flash of light illuminated the fog. Then the aliens were gone. Madame Pompeii scanned the outskirts and saw them standing to the side. Movie magic. All smoke and mirrors.

On the other side of the fog she could see the outline of Howard talking to his little friend. The mist cleared for a moment and a third figure appeared, leaning against a walker and holding an oblong bag. Grady's acquaintance, the man she'd encountered downtown. Well, she had a few words for him after he'd electrocuted her.

Madame Pompeii skirted around the scene, batting at the fog as she went. All the while, she kept her eyes trained on the trio. That atrocious man owed her an explanation. All she'd done was reach out in a friendly gesture and gotten a hearty jolt of electricity in return. Had he somehow done it on purpose, or was it the result of a powerful spiritual connection? Anyway, he should have apologized when she screamed. Such rude behavior.

She lifted the hem of her muumuu to step over a tangle of cable strewn across the street, glancing up to keep her sights on the three figures. Howard was shaking hands with the old man and that odd little boy.

Without warning, another flash of light filled the fog, making her squint. When she opened her eyes again, only Howard stood there. Alone.

Another trick of light and mirrors? She snapped her attention to the spot where the earlier aliens on the set had reappeared. But now no one stood there at all. She scanned the rest of the location but saw no sign of the man and hooded child.

After elbowing her way past spectators and film crew, she finally reached Howard. "Where are your friends?"

"They went home."

"Home? But they were just standing here."

"That's how it works. They come. They go. They live in another dementia."

"Do you mean dimension?"

Howard just stared at her.

* * *

Pleasance pulled herself up from the pillow and looked at the alarm clock. One-thirty – that had to be P.M. Light shone through the open bedroom window.

She'd been dreaming about gun shots – first coming from The Three Fools but then from Winchester's henchman. Cap stood to the side, doing nothing. She'd been dodging bullets as she dashed through dense jungle vegetation. Leaping over a hundred-foot-wide cenoté filled with chickens, she landed on something warm and pudgy. Buford Price. *Can I buy you dinner?* he asked. Breathless, she explained that she couldn't because all she had to wear was a wetsuit. She looked down at her outfit, a laced corset and black leather hot pants that barely covered her butt. Below that, fishnet stockings disappeared into tall, stiletto boots.

She slapped a riding crop against her thigh and barked at Buford, *This is Honeysuckle, and this is what's going to happen to you.*

At that point, Buford morphed into a large-headed alien and began shooting at her with a toy gun.

Pop! Pop! Pop!

But she was awake now, and she still heard the sound. Coming from outside.

Pleasance kicked off the sheet and staggered over to the window. Across the backyard she saw her aunt banging a hammer against the two-by-four frame of her half-finished coop. Lela dropped the tool and yanked hard on chicken wire attached to the boards. Half the enclosure collapsed to the ground.

Through the screen, Pleasance shouted, "Whatcha doing, Aunt Lela?"

The woman paused and called over her shoulder, "I'm tearing this damn thing down."

"Why?"

"Because it's a chicken coop."

"But where will the chickens live?"

Lela stomped over to the window. "I hate those filthy things. They smell and poop all over the grass."

Pleasance stammered, "But you – you and your friends love chickens."

"Loved. Past tense. I don't know what I was thinking." She turned back toward the shambles of wire and wood to continue her work.

Pleasance pulled on her bathrobe and padded down the hall into the kitchen. At the table sat Perry, sipping a cup of coffee. She poured her own and slumped into the chair beside him.

"Good morning, Uncle Perry."

He nodded as he devoured a piece of toast slathered with cream cheese.

"Aunt Lela is tearing down her chicken coop," she said.

"Yeah, and all her friends are, too."

Maybe she should have shown more interest in this latest turn of events, but Pleasance had more pressing things on her mind.

"Sort of a rough night, wasn't it?" she ventured.

He looked up and grinned. "Yeah, but a helluva lot of fun."

"Not much to show for it."

* * *

The sun had already reached the recesses of the arroyo that morning when they had regained consciousness at the foot of the cave. Maurice was long gone, of course, taking the treasure with him. Mocoso and Lorenzo still lay like sleeping babies on the rocks.

On the drive back home, Perry couldn't stop talking. Apparently, the whole experience had done nothing but energize him. By contrast, Pleasance had just stared ahead at the road. How was she going to make good on the deal she'd made with Winchester now? Everything had depended on this score. The worst part was that she had the treasure in her hands before The Three Fools and then Maurice had snatched it away.

Her burning anger at the previous night's events now cooled into icy anxiety. With the treasure gone, she needed to come up with a new exit plan, and quick.

She tipped the coffee mug and drained it.

The banging of the front door thrown open interrupted her descent into self-pity. She heard Madame Pompeii puffing toward the kitchen.

"I saw the most amazing thing today," the psychic said. She glanced at both Pleasance and Perry. "You two just getting up?"

"It's a long story," Pleasance began.

"Never mind. Let me tell you what happened to me this morning." She sat down, picked up a napkin, and dabbed her forehead. Her pasted star stuck to the paper. "I saw two people disappear, just like that!' She snapped her fingers.

Pleasance didn't feel like listening to her aunt's newest tale, and she bet Perry didn't either. While her aunt babbled about her experience at the film shoot, Pleasance began making mental notes about her next course of action. She needed to get back to New York and find Maurice. His brownstone would be hard to break into, but she had to recover those artifacts for Winchester. Maybe she'd even help herself to a few other things at the same time. He'd certainly stolen enough from her.

"– and then he was gone," Madame Pompeii said. "Him, the kid, the bag, and the walker. All gone. Poof!"

Pleasance's head snapped in her aunt's direction. "Did you say 'walker'?"

"Yes. Why?"

"You mean you just saw Maurice? An old man with a walker?"

"I didn't know his name, but yes, I've seen him around town the past couple of weeks with Mr. O'Grady."

"Where did you see him?"

"That's what I've been telling you. At the film shoot. One minute he was standing there next to Howard Beacon, and the next instant, he'd disappeared." She paused and laughed. "Howard said he was an inter-dimensional traveler."

Pleasance grabbed Perry's forearm. "He must be the one Grady made the deal with. I've got to catch a plane back home tonight."

"The next flight doesn't leave until this evening." Perry stood. "I'll call and see if I can get us on it."

"Uh-uh, not this time, Uncle Perry. If things go wrong, it might be a little harder to get you out of a New York jail."

Perry looked disappointed but nodded. He got on the phone while Pleasance ran to hop in the shower.

* * *

In all the excitement, Madame Pompeii hadn't the chance to tell them her other news. She left the kitchen, collected the birdcage, and walked right past that dreadful, worthless cat. She got in her car and backed out of the driveway. On her way through town, she had to brake several times to avoid hitting flocks of loose chickens, dragging unattended leashes. No one paid much attention to them. One bystander even threw rocks at one, and not a single person on the sidewalk ran to its rescue.

Madame Pompeii wasn't sure how she'd broken the curse, but her paranormal powers must have been greater than she ever imagined.

Telemarketing Enterprises came into view, and she turned into the parking lot.

Pat Montgomery hadn't been too keen on her counter-proposal when she'd gone to see him after the film shoot that morning.

"Well, I don't know if I like that idea," he'd told her. "I think you can do *this* job. They'll still think you're a hot chick." He paused and pointed at her muumuu. "No matter what you look like."

No, he didn't like her idea, but he was desperate and it didn't take much to convince him to set up an additional option on the voice menu.

She parked the car and entered the building, waving at Pat as she walked to her cubicle. He had shown her the ropes that morning after they'd made their deal. She set the caged parrot on the desk and sat down, pulling on the headset.

"Ready, Pandora?"

"Take a trip, take a trip," her familiar squawked.

The psychic pushed a blinking light on the phone.

"This is Madame Pompeii, and this is what's going to happen to you. I see a trip in your future …"

* * *

It'd been a busy morning. Grady woke up to the sound of the old Chrysler roaring out of his driveway, carrying his three new hands. The bunkhouse had been empty with no sign of Maurice either. First thing he did was drive out to the digging site, where he found fresh tire tracks and a lot more footprints than there should have been. He crawled up the hill into the cave but saw no evidence of coins or any other artifacts.

He'd slapped his knee and whooped. Everything had worked out the way he'd hoped. The treasure was now in the hands of outsiders and they were probably long gone.

Silverville's luck couldn't have been better.

And now he could get back to the daily chores. He still needed to mend some fence in the north pasture and separate those baby beefalo from their mamas.

He walked into the kitchen. Leona stood in the middle of the room, just untying her scarf.

"I heard something at Bible study this morning that you ought to know."

Grady dropped his hat on the table. His own news could wait.

"Lela might be arrested for kidnapping Bob Hardin and Arno Aasfresser. Looks like she may have been part of that chicken gang."

"That so?"

"Grady O'Grady, you march right into town and clear this mess up. It's time you told Carl what you know."

"Chores need tending first."

Scarf still in hand, she pointed toward the door, her lips flat and thin with determination. She gave him *that look.*

No use arguing with Leona once that happened. He picked up his hat and climbed back in his pickup. Once he got to town, Grady saw chickens running rampant through the streets.

The curse was broken.

He parked the truck in front of the Lazy S diner, next to the sheriff's SUV. As he passed through the door, Arno blustered out, nearly knocking him down. The man carried a long pole attached to a net under his arm. Grady stepped aside to let him pass and moseyed into the restaurant. The rancher spotted Carl in the booth that the sheriff always occupied that time of day. Grady dropped into the seat opposite him.

"Afternoon, Grady. Buy you a cup of coffee?"

"That's neighborly of you."

The waitress set a cup of coffee in front of Grady.

"You want a slice of pie with that?" she asked.

He shook his head and she left.

"Where was Arno off to in such a hurry?" he asked Carl.

"Didn't you see all those damn chickens? Someone's got to catch them."

"Yeah, I need to talk to you about that."

Grady told the sheriff about his experience as a kid, the curse, the reappearance of the coins. Next, he told him how he'd managed to get the tainted treasure out of Silverville. With Maurice and the artifacts gone, the curse was over.

"And that's why you see all them abandoned chickens," Grady finished. "Nobody wants 'em anymore."

Carl nearly choked on his coffee. "Well, I knew something strange was going on in town, but if somebody else had told me it was a bona fide curse, I wouldn't have believed it."

"You gotta drop charges against Lela. She ain't responsible for her actions."

Carl pushed his hat off his forehead and whistled. "You got a good point there. I think we need to run this past Earl Bob. Under the circumstances, I think he'll agree."

* * *

Lela gathered the last pile of boards and wire into the wheelbarrow and started for the dumpster in the alley.

Perry poked his head out the kitchen door. "Sure I can't help you with the last of that?"

Lela shook her head. Twice that afternoon she'd chased him out of the yard when he tried to help her. She was the one who had created this mess – even though it was the curse that had compelled her. Now she was the one who needed to clean it up.

She dropped the last pieces of the coop into the dumpster, returned the wheelbarrow to the garage, and headed back to the house.

Once inside, she pulled off her gloves and glanced at the kitchen clock. "Getting close to supper time," she said to Perry. "Tamale TV dinners okay?"

"Don't make one for Pleasance. She's getting ready to leave for the airport."

Lela paused and turned toward her husband. "What?"

"Long story. I'll tell you after she goes."

As if on cue, Pleasance walked out of her bedroom, carrying two suitcases.

"Does this have something to do with you two getting home in the wee hours of the morning?" Lela scolded. "You didn't think I noticed, but I did. What are you guys up to?"

Pleasance set the suitcases down and hugged her. "Nothing, Aunt Lela. Just a sudden change of plans."

Lela didn't believe that for a minute. By the look of Perry's bruised knuckles, there had been more of an adventure the previous night than they were letting on. "I think you both better 'fess up."

Lela didn't have a chance to continue. Pleasance reached into her pocket and produced a hand-sized amulet in the shape of a bird, decorated with seashells.

"This is for you," Pleasance said. "It's a buzzard. A sign of hope and change to the Mayan people."

As Lela turned the bird over in her hand, her niece told her the story. "Their culture has its own flood myth. Only instead of a dove bringing back an olive branch, it's a buzzard smelling of carrion."

"Thank you ... I guess."

"It seemed appropriate. Wasn't your maiden name Buzzard?"

"No!" Lela answered in an automatic reaction. "It was BuzZARD."

Pleasance looked puzzled for a moment and continued, "Whatever. Anyway, I brought this back from Mexico and wanted you to have it."

"That was thoughtful of you." Lela set the BuzZARD on the counter. "But Pleasance, I'm concerned about you dashing off on the spur of the moment. I know Perry's enjoyed your visit."

"Thanks. I enjoyed it, too. Well, I still have my carry-on to pack." Pleasance went back to her bedroom.

Perry picked up the bird amulet and studied it. "A nice little sign of her appreciation."

A sign, yes. Perhaps he was right. Perhaps the buzzard signaled a need for hope and change for *her*. Lela had already gotten the first of her wishes, that the haunting – which she later learned was part of the curse – would end. Maybe it was now time to consider her second wish, a better last name. Buzzard wasn't really her idea of a better last name, but Pleasance's gift seemed to be telling her that she should own up to who she was. A Buzzard. For the Mayans, that meant the hope for dry land and a change from disaster. For Lela, it would be a different kind of change.

"Perry, what you think about me switching my last name back to Buzzard?"

* * *

Billfold, passport, toothbrush. Too many times had Pleasance found herself without a means of brushing her teeth when her luggage didn't arrive on the same plane as she did. She stuffed the three items into her carry-on luggage.

Since she didn't have her old apartment to return to, she'd have to check in at a hotel, preferably one close to Maurice's brownstone. That old bastard.

She made one final sweep through the bedroom to make sure she hadn't forgotten any of her things. In between the dresser and bed leaned a cardboard tube. Her first inclination was that it belonged to Lela, but why hadn't she noticed it before? Pleasance set her bag down and hefted the tube. Very light, still sealed in its package. Along the side, scrawled in black felt pen, read "For Pleasance."

Her heart warmed at the thought of Perry and Lela giving her a going-away gift. She peeled off the end cap and withdrew a rolled-up sheath. A small slip of paper fell at her feet, which she plucked up.

Hand-written were the words, "For the love of our game. xxoo, M." A familiar purple candy wafer was taped to the note.

Puzzled by the cryptic message, she scrabbled to unroll what turned out to be a canvas. Her breath froze in mid exhale.

She held in her hands one of the two original Delacroix *épreuves d'artist* that Maurice had hustled from her in Berlin, an initial drawing of a fractious Arab stallion that would figure in the famous painting, *The Moroccan and his Horse*. The sketch could be worth millions.

Pleasance collapsed onto the bed, trying to slow her breathing. Why would Maurice do this? Had all her crazy dealings with him been just a game? To her, his interference had often been devastating, the current episode at the cave dangerous. And the consequences could end in Winchester's deadly wrath. She would take the sketch and decide later whether or not to feel gratitude towards Maurice.

The value of the Delacroix work would far exceed her debt to Winchester. They would easily cancel Cap's debt as well.

On a long shot, she fished out the cell that Cap had given her and dialed his number. He wouldn't be there, of course, but she'd leave a message to call.

"Hello, Pleasance."

"Is this a recording?"

"No, it's really me. I'd hoped to hear from you."

"You – you, have?" Why did he even answer the phone? He was supposed to be hiding out. "Never mind, this has gotta be quick."

She told him about her discovery of the sketch and how it might buy the both of them out of their scrape with Winchester.

"Is it stolen goods?"

What difference would it make to Cap? "Of course. It's black market. Gotta run. I'm on my way to catch a flight to take it to Winchester right now."

"Pleasance, listen to me carefully. This is what we're going to do."

* * *

From the living room, the doorbell sounded. A few seconds later, Aunt Lela peeked into the bedroom just as Pleasance snapped the cell phone shut.

"There's a man at the front door who wants to speak to you."

Must be the cab driver. She'd returned the rental that afternoon and decided to say her goodbyes at the house. But the cab wasn't supposed to come for another thirty minutes.

"Tell him I'll be right there." She zipped up her carry-on, tucked the tube under her arm, and walked into the living room where Lela and Perry waited.

"Thank you so much for everything," Pleasance said and hugged them each in turn.

"You come back real soon," Perry told her. "Remember Tunisia!"

Pleasance hefted a suitcase under her arm and opened the door.

Before her stood a man with a large bandage wrapping the top of his head. Blackened eyes perched above a swollen and crooked nose.

At the same time that her eyes traveled down to his gold lip ring, he reached inside his jacket and began to pull out something that bulged beneath his upper arm.

Pleasance froze. "Don't shoot! I've got something for Winchester!"

* * *

Pleasance sat in the austere room, waiting. Winchester's secretary busied herself sorting folders in the file cabinet beside her desk. How many other indentured freelancers did the man employ? And how many of those folders contained obituaries for closed accounts?

Something sour pushed into her throat, and she gulped to shove it back down. The moisture from her hands left sweaty imprints on the tube she clutched. She glanced at the clock on the wall. Twenty minutes had passed while she fidgeted in the overstuffed chair. He was deliberately making her wait, a power play to demonstrate his control. Or maybe to give her time to imagine all the things he might do to her if he disliked what she brought him.

The goons would be in the inner office, of course. She wondered if they carried concealed weapons. Probably. They wouldn't be the only ones with something hidden under their clothes. She twisted uncomfortably against the foreign feel of her own concealment.

Her thoughts turned to Uncle Perry and their many earlier escapades. Some with narrow escapes. She'd always managed to keep her cool, no matter how dicey the circumstances. But this time was different. If things didn't go as planned, would Perry and Lela mourn her? Would they bring her body – if they could find it – back to Silverville for burial? And she might never have a chance to thank Maurice for his gesture, the old bastard.

She thought of her night in the Placer City hotel with Cap. If she only lived through the next hour, she might be able to take him back there someday. Or maybe even to the Galactic Inn.

A buzzer sounded on the desk. Without even looking up, the secretary announced, "You can go in now."

Pleasance stood, cleared her throat, made a show to straighten her back with a self-confidence she didn't feel, and marched toward the door. She reached for the ornate brass of the knob, but the door swung open, and one of the goons curtly gestured her inside.

Winchester sat behind his desk.

She walked up and presented him with the tube. For a moment, arms folded, he studied the tube as though he wouldn't accept her offering. But at last he reached out and took it.

"Seems light for Spanish artifacts," he said, rotating the package with his fingers. "And rather small."

Pleasance licked dry lips and glanced from one goon to the other, who now stood on either side of her. "It's not a Spanish artifact. Silverville was a bust. I made another deal."

Winchester frowned as he opened the tube and withdrew the contents. "What have we here?"

He spread the rolled canvas across his desk, anchoring the curled corners with paperweights. Opening the drawer in front of him, he pulled out a loupe, bent over, and held it to his eye.

While he studied the canvas, Pleasance blurted, "It's a Delacroix." *Too nervous, slow down.*

Winchester pored over the sketch for a full five minutes before finally turning to Pleasance. "Explain."

"It's one of the preliminary sketches the artist made for *The Moroccan and his Horse*. The work is authentic."

"Did you think I couldn't tell?" Winchester's voice sounded indignant.

"No, no, of course not."

He returned his attention to the sketch. It seemed like hours passed before he removed the paperweights, rolled the sketch back up, and replaced it in the tube.

It looked like he wasn't interested. In her haste to get him something, she might have overestimated its worth. No, it was a Delacroix. The sketch should have more than satisfied him. Yet he just sat there, not speaking, turning his to chair to gaze out the window.

She couldn't stand it.

"So, are we square? You going to take it?"

He swiveled his chair back in her direction, steepled his fingers, and sighed. In a soft, almost hushed tone, he said, "Yes."

Pleasance panicked. She could barely hear him. "Can you say that a little louder?"

With a look of disgust, he barked, "Yes, of course, I'll take –"

He stopped short, realization clouding his face.

"She's wearing a wire! Search her, boys."

The two goons pounced on Pleasance. At the same moment, the office door exploded open. Cap, flanked by six burly men, charged into the room, guns raised and pointed at Winchester and his henchmen.

"Federal agents! On the floor, hands behind your heads," Cap shouted.

Winchester and the goons didn't have time to comply. The agents man-handled all three to the carpet and cuffed them. Cap stepped over the bodies and pulled guns from the goons' pockets. "You're charged with trafficking illegal art."

While the other agents read them their Miranda rights, Cap turned to Pleasance. "You did just fine. You okay?"

"Yeah."

Pleasance realized she'd been holding her breath for the past two minutes and exhaled, deeply. Lots of things could have gone wrong. Winchester might have refused the sketch. His goons might have had time to toss her out the window. When the Feds came through the door, the scene might have turned into a gunfight. But she needn't have worried – everything worked out just as Cap planned. When she'd phoned him just after discovering Maurice's gift, Pleasance had been stunned when she learned that, all along, he'd been a Federal agent working undercover. But she was grateful he'd given her a chance to be part of the sting team, rather than lying on the floor in cuffs now.

She reached under her shirt to tear off the taped wire and microphone.

"Here, let me help." Cap turned her around and unfastened the transmitter.

In the meantime, the other agents herded the three captives out of the office into the waiting room. She and Cap followed.

At the desk sat the irritating secretary, hands bound to the chair arms and mouth gagged with a broad strip of tape. Her eyes were wide with fear.

"You're coming, too," Cap said.

He walked over to cut the straps securing the woman.

Pleasance stepped in front of him and took the knife. "Let me do it."

In one powerful yank, she ripped the flat gag from the secretary's mouth, not apologizing for all the whiskers clinging to the back of the tape.

* * *

At the curbside below Winchester's building, Pleasance stood to the side while the Feds escorted the captives into a waiting black SUV.

Cap turned to her. "If we're going to have a relationship, you need to find a better line of work."

Pleasance smiled. "Don't worry. I learned my lesson."

EPILOGUE

Brush snapped under her feet as she waded over the dense jungle floor. Clawing through branches and vines, Pleasance struggled to place more distance between her and her pursuers. Mud clutched the soles of her boots, pitching her forward into a wall of ferns that tangled in her hair and tore at her braids. The fall thrust her face in close proximity to what looked like a night-hunting fer de lance – the most deadly snake in the Yucatán. She scrambled to her feet and kept running.

Behind her, angry voices filtered through the vegetation, getting ever closer. Mocoso and his band navigated the rainforest maze with the practiced ease of *indios* used to such terrain, making it harder for her to stay ahead of them. To the right, her eyes caught the reflection of the moon's glare off the damp earth of a narrow animal trail. She dodged down the path, running ten yards before it gave way to a steep embankment. And then she was on her back sliding out of control. The revolver tore from her belt as she dug her heels into the slick mud of a long, sloping hill, fighting to slow her descent. When she reached the bottom, her boots lodged against a low rock outcropping. She struggled to her feet to see the moon shining off a pool of water far below her. A cenoté, its edges rimmed with roots and tree vines that disappeared off the bank and into the watery abyss.

Curses and shouts told her that The Three Fools were now also plunging down the hill. No time to hesitate. She reached for a vine and launched off the edge of the cenoté. She swung blindly into the dark over the bottomless pit of water. For a moment, she sailed across the abyss, but the top of the vine snagged on a limb, suspending her over the well. At that moment, her cell phone began ringing.

"Damn!" she muttered. She wound one arm tighter around the vine so she could free the other to grope in her pocket for the phone. But her fingers were too caked with mud to turn off the ringer. She threw the phone into the well.

Just as it hit the water, the higher branch hooking her vine broke, and she dropped a dozen feet. The jolt of the drop sent the vine arcing backward toward the hill and The Three Fools, and she slammed into the limestone side of the cenoté. Her grip loosened and she slid down the vine into the pit. Before she reached the water, she landed on a narrow ledge. Pleasance crouched down and hugged the wall to stay in the shadows, so the men wouldn't discover her exact location.

Flashlight beams danced over the vertical rock, but a fringe of dangling roots prevented her pursuers from seeing where she was.

Soon the echo of Mocoso's voice reverberated through the cavernous pit. *"Señorita!* You think the vine save you? How long before you fall?"

Still crouching on the ledge, she stood and her foot struck a loose block of limestone.

"Your friend escapes, but not you."

She finagled the heavy block from its resting place and lifted it above her head. She shouted, "I can't hold on! Help me, I can't swim!" Pleasance screamed as she hurled the boulder into the pool. Immediately, the flashlights angled on the splashing ripples that radiated across the cenoté.

"Cut!" a voice shouted from the edge of the cliff above.

* * *

A long array of lights burst from the scaffolding attached to the roof of the immense hangar, and the scene blanched into reality. Well, the backstage reality of a movie set.

One of the crew members dropped a ladder down the constructed cliff wall, so Pleasance could climb out. At the top, someone handed her a towel and congratulated her on a good day's work.

The Three Fools stood along the side, Mocoso offering her a beer.

"Close call, eh, *amiga*?" he said. "You almost miss the mattress when you drop onto the cenoté ledge."

"Whew! You're right about that."

They all laughed.

She continued, "Well, boys. Another day, another dollar. See ya tomorrow."

They shook hands all around, and she walked toward the hangar door.

Antoine Marcus caught her before she could leave. The black around his eyes had already faded from a deep purple to a puke yellow. She could even see the gold ring a little better now that his lip wasn't as swollen.

"I knew I had a good hunch about you," he said. "Your stunts are dynamite."

"Thanks." She ducked past him, still feeling a little sheepish about setting him up with those cowboys at the bar. But how could she have known that he was the executive producer for Creative Solutions Film Company?

That last day at Uncle Perry's, she nearly decked him at the door when he'd reached into his jacket. She'd been sure he was Winchester's thug and about to pull out a gun. Instead, the only thing he shot at her was an acting contract for an upcoming adventure film.

From that moment, her luck changed. She now had a steady income. A lucrative one at that, thanks to the Screen Actors Guild.

Waving at Mr. Marcus and his assistant, Candace Good, she slipped through the hangar door and met Cap, where he usually waited. They hadn't quite made it to the parking lot and her new Mustang convertible, when four actors in vampire make-up intercepted her.

"Excuse me," one of them said. "Is your name Honeysuckle?"

She paused in mid-stride. "Yes. No! What did you say?"

"Your pimp just booked you for the night with us." He held out his hand. "He said to give you this."

The vampire actor dropped a small purple Pez wafer into her palm.

Pleasance looked at the candy and scanned the parking lot and nearby sets. She thought she caught a glimpse of a metal walker disappearing around the corner of a building.

She raised her fist and shook it.

"Maurice, you old bastard!"

The End
(Perhaps)

READ ON
To see an excerpt from
"Little Greed Men."

This was originally published by Ghost Road Press of Denver, CO as "The Silverville Swindle," Book One of the Silverville Saga.

Watch for its re-issue, coming soon from Raspberry Creek Books.

And stay tuned for a potential Book Three of the Silverville Saga.

What could possibly happen in our favorite mountain town this time?

An excerpt from
Little Greed Men
(formerly The Silverville Swindle)
a novel by Kym O'Connell-Todd and Mark Todd

Prolog

Earl Bob Jackson had to piss. How was he to know it would be his last act on Earth?

He squinted into his windshield trying to see past the stripes of snow that glanced off his yellow Cadillac DeVille. The headlights managed to illuminate a ten-foot path in front of his vehicle, but beyond that, he could only guess what the terrain looked like. He was on a mountain pass – this much he knew – and although he sometimes felt like the car moved downhill, Earl Bob didn't think he had yet reached the summit.

"This road sucks," he muttered to himself. "This weather sucks. Colorado sucks."

What was worse, his bladder felt like a bloated dead cow about to explode in the sun. He'd seen plenty of those, although most of them, or what was left, rotted in the wake of mysterious circumstance. Cored rectums. Surgically excised lips. The usual stuff that accompanied mutilations.

Take that time he investigated the mass "murder" of a herd of calves in Ten Sheep, Wyoming. Those ranchers were mad as hell by the time they'd called him in. Whoever, or whatever, performed the work had really done a fine job. Earl Bob had found the calves picked with a clean precision. Not only were their rectums and lips gone, everything but the skeletons had been removed, leaving the bones as intact as a museum exhibit. No predators could have managed such a tidy scene. And no satanic cult would have taken the trouble. Besides, no one found footprints, just a patch of burnt sagebrush and grass nearby.

Why did his work always seem to take him to the middle of nowhere? Earl Bob unclenched one fist from the steering wheel, flexing his fingers. The radio vacillated between "Your Cheatin' Heart" and an irritating hum, punctuated with occasional blasts of

Mexican mariachi music, depending on the turn of the road. But this late at night, he was willing to listen to whatever he could find. He dared not take his attention from the snow-packed pavement to fumble for his collection of gospel CDs. Fat fingers of snow reached across the highway in front of him, the wheels thumping each drift with a soft shudder that resonated in his bladder.

If this was springtime in the Rockies, Earl Bob wasn't impressed. This was nothing like the picture that joker from Silverville had painted for him on the phone. He hoped that Buford Price's promises of success would be more accurate than his predictions about Colorado weather.

Earl Bob recalled bits and pieces of those promises: . . . *we've got a project that needs somebody with your kind of credentials . . . a good money-making venture . . . make it worth your while . . . pay all your expenses . . .*

It was true. They did need Earl Bob's expertise to pull off this scheme. Besides, he was tired of working for government wages, tired of getting shuffled all over the country. Tired of exposing the UFO hoaxes of publicity-starved amateurs. Not that Silverville's plan wasn't the same thing, but if the town was going to cash in on what everyone wanted to hear, then maybe it was time for Earl Bob to cash in, too.

He'd never miss those jerks in the investigative department. They didn't even give him a going-away party. Twenty years in government service was enough.

Now that cute little piece, Judy, was a different story. There were nights between road trips when he had enjoyed her company. He found himself telling her about his investigations, his problems, his complaints. Judy always listened as he settled his head against her soft bosom; he took comfort from her caresses and quiet words of sympathy. Earl Bob told Judy lots of things he never told anyone else. Things like how he had trouble urinating in public bathrooms. Like how he colored his hair to disguise the early signs of graying.

He had even told Judy about The Secret. How, as a reckless young driver in his boyhood home in Tennessee, he had once struck down a teenager at a crosswalk. Earl Bob had kept right on going, something he had never confessed to anyone – except, of course, Judy.

But when she moved her answering machine into his apartment, things began to look too permanent. He was too old to start a family, too old for that kind of commitment. There would be other women like Judy in Silverville. If he ever managed to get there.

He glanced at the clock in the dash. 2:00 a.m. He hadn't seen another car for over an hour and a half, and he suspected that no one but a fool would be out so late on a night like this. Not this early on a Monday morning. It began to snow harder, and his visibility shrunk to the point that the world around him was no more than a small dark room. A room with no toilet.

The wipers labored to push wet snow off the windshield, leaving an ever-diminishing hole for him to peer at the road. Earl Bob decided he might as well stop, clean the glass, and piss at the same time. He eased to a stop, not daring to pull to the side of the road since there was no telling where it started or ended. He left the engine running and the headlights on.

He pushed the door against the wind and felt wet slushy pellets splatter onto his face and hair as he wedged his beefy body out into the night. But when his slick-soled wingtips touched the snow, they slipped out from under him and sent Earl Bob into a graceless pitch forward onto his hands and knees.

"Son-of-a-bitch," Earl Bob muttered as he struggled to his feet and fumbled with the pants zipper. He stopped short as he noticed a swelling light over his shoulder. His eyes turned in the direction of the glow, which seemed to hover just above the snow-packed road with an eerie, bluish cast.

"Mother of God!" he gasped.

The glow quickly enveloped his entire body, tracing the silhouette of a small man with wet pants, and an empty bladder.

(What the *bleep* is going on? Watch for "Little Greed Men" coming soon!)

ABOUT THE AUTHORS

Kym O'Connell-Todd is a writer and graphic designer.
Mark Todd is a college professor and program director for
Western State Colorado University's MFA in Creative
Writing. They live in the Cochetopa Mountains east of
Gunnison with more animals than most reasonable people
would feed.

Visit the authors' Web site at www.writeinthethick.com

CPSIA information can be obtained at www.ICGtesting.com
Printed in the USA
BVOW011701040213

312358BV00007B/63/P

9 780985 135218